Voices in the Ghost Light

Mark Greene

Dedicated to Saliha, who listens to all our stories.

Voices in the Ghost Light
Published by ThinkPlay Partners
ISBN: 979-8-9870246-3-8
©2025 by Mark Greene
All Rights Reserved

Table of Contents

Chapter 1

A woman sat in a pool of light cast from a single reading lamp. She held a cigarette in one still hand, smoke drifting up untroubled by any current of air, disappearing into the blackness beyond the light of the lamp. Next to her was an ashtray, overflowing. Dozens of cigarette butts pinched out in a sea of ash. A scrap of glistening cellophane lay curled on the side table next to a pack of cigarettes and a cell phone.

The fingertips of her free hand brushed her lips, searching for the tiny sliver of fingernail she had just bitten off. She found it and plucked it away, examining it between her fingers. The whites of her fingernails were long gone. Red stubs, raw and tender, remained. She continued to examine her work, taking a drag off her cigarette. The cigarette's red tip glowed as she inhaled, a light audible hiss in the absolute silence, falling quiet as she exhaled.

She sat on a couch in a breakfast nook at one end of a long dark kitchen. Beyond the kitchen table, the basement door was in her line of sight. She was in her mid-thirties. She had pale skin and dark curly hair, cut short. Her eyes where dark brown. Exhaustion made her hand movements sloppy. The cigarette rising to her lips, bumped them, sending an ash tumbling into her lap. She brushed it away. Her eyes drifted closed. The ash on the cigarette began to lengthen. Minutes ticked by.

As she drowsed, the basement door gently swung open, coming to a halt against a raised spot on the linoleum floor. The woman startled awake. Again the ash parted and fell to her lap. She did not brush it away. She lowered the cigarette to the ashtray and stubbed it out, shifting to sit upright on the couch to present herself to the open door, marshaling her courage.

She wore a thick bath robe over a sweatshirt and sweatpants. She pulled her robe closer about her, peering into the well of darkness the led down into the basement, her lips jerked down at the edges, her expression resolving into a hard grimace.

She heard whispering, faint at first, like sheets of paper moving lightly against each other. Her instinct was to freeze, unmoving. She resisted the urge. Not taking her eyes off the basement door, she reached out her hand and felt across the top of the table for her cell phone. She located it and started recording audio. She held it out, her lips pulling back off her teeth.

The whispering came in waves, rising and falling like a radio tuning in some signal over a great distance. It was a foreign tongue. Unfamiliar. There were many different voices, some high, others lower, some urgent and filled with panic. Then abruptly, the voices stopped. Minutes passed; she lowered the phone.

By feel, she found her cigarettes on the side table. She took the lighter from the pocket of her robe, lit a new cigarette, and placed the lighter back into the pocket. She settled back into the couch and watched the doorway impassively, the silence broken only by the occasional hiss of the cigarette. After a time, she began to relax.

There was the clear, bright creak of a footfall on the basement stairs. Something was faintly visible against the deeper blackness.

She took another long draw on the cigarette, her hand trembling. On the couch to her right was a flashlight. By feel, she located it and picked it up. There was a click as she turned it on and trained the light on the doorway of the basement. A shoulder and part of a man's face was visible, pale and ghastly in the beam of the flashlight. He was old and haggard, worn down by long illness. He stood with one hand on the basement rail, the other hung at his side, unmoving. His face wore an expression of utter exhaustion. His one visible pupil was cataract-white, like ice. The door slammed violently closed.

Chapter 2

The golden light of mid-morning lanced into the kitchen, throwing an arc of warm color across the wall. Her cell phone rang. The woman woke with a start. She rose, examining the phone, seeing the name of the caller. The room, now revealed in the daylight, was a confusion of take-out boxes and dirty dishes.

"Hello, Marty," she said.

"Ellen?" said a man's voice.

The woman sighed, her body sagging visibly. She pushed her curly hair back out of her face.

"Yes, Marty," she replied.

"Sorry but I really had to call," the man said.

"It's fine," she said.

"Ellen, I know it's been tough, with your father and all, but it's been two months, and we want you to come out and have lunch with us or something."

"I know, I know, and I will," she replied, pulling her robe closed and beginning to tidy up around the couch as if her situation was visible to the man on the phone.

"Ellen, you're a therapist. You know what we're all thinking. We're thinking this isolation isn't good for you. And you know, at some point we'll come to you if we have to."

Ellen smiled. "I know, Marty. But not just yet, all right?"

He pressed on. "Ellen, seriously, we want to see you, to see how you're doing. Soon."

Ellen reached for the cigarettes.

"Okay, good. How about next week?" she said, taking one from the pack.

"How about his week?"

"Marty."

"Okay, MONDAY next week. We'll just come get you. We'll have lunch. Anna's coming."

"I'll let you know."

"Monday, Ellen. Noon."

"Fine. Great. Thank you, Marty.

"Thank you, Ellen."

She smiled again, grimacing.

"I'm going to make you pay for this, Marty."

"Don't I know it," Marty said.

Ellen hung up the phone, and rose from the couch, glancing toward the basement door. She walked down the long hallway towards the front of the house. Passing by, she saw her face in the mirror that hung there. It was manic and ragged with exhaustion.

She went up the stairs, heading to the bathroom, passing the doorway of her father's room. The room was awash in sunlight. There was a mechanical hospital bed with metal side rails. The sheets had been stripped off, leaving the plastic-covered mattress. His television was there on a stand at the foot of the bed. She looked down at the television's plug disconnected on the floor. The hospital bed should have been returned months ago but she couldn't yet accept anyone entering the house, no matter how briefly.

Over the last year, during her father's illness, she had become intimately familiar with the voices of all the ESPN commentators, sounding tinny through the hissing baby monitor she kept next to her bed in her room down the hall. It had been her bedroom as a child. Being in it again had brought back all the powerlessness of childhood. It was coupled with the immense challenges of caring for her father. His terminal illness offered no timeline, no predictability, no respite, no clarity, no control. Caring for him meant giving over control of her life in the most fundamental way.

During his long illness, the late-night sports wrap-up continued until well after midnight. ESPN was her father's sole comfort in the darkness. He would call out to her to turn him or help him relieve himself. Using the sheet to pull him onto his side, she would stand next to his bed in the darkened house, holding the urine bottle and listening for the decrease in flow, the intermittent roar of the stadium crowds on the TV, her expression neutral in the glow of the screen.

She continued down the hall to the bathroom. She took a toothbrush from the holder. As she put toothpaste on it, she heard the TV in her father's room come to life. She slowly closed the bathroom door and began brushing her teeth vigorously. As the TV warmed up, the sound rose; commentators talking college football. The volume rose to a roar.

Her resolve to ignore the TV faltered. She turned her head slightly toward the sound, the toothbrush dangling in her hand, a snarl forming on her lips. Foam dribbled freely down her chin and into the sink. The bathroom filled with a smell. The bitter smell of urine and the sickly-sweet stink of human waste. Something bumped lightly against the door. Angry tears began to stream down her face, falling trembling into the sink.

Abruptly, she swung to face the door. "Go away!" she

screamed, battering the door with her fists, chest, and shoulders. When she finally stopped, the house was silent. She turned back to the sink, her hands dangling at her side. Then, she raised the toothbrush and continued brushing her teeth.

Chapter 3

The San Francisco bar was something from another era, its better days decades past. Trash had blown up around the little, inset doorway. Window shades blocked her view inside. Ellen looked at the address on her phone, then glanced at the address on a garage across the street. Collecting herself, she turned the door handle and entered.

It took a few seconds for her eyes to adjust to the gloom. There was the sickly-sweet smell of stale beer. The bartender to her left was washing glasses. She took a few steps toward him. Grey-haired and sallow-eyed, he raised his chin toward the back of the room.

Ellen turned. There was only one person in the bar. He sat in a booth, a puddle of riotous sunlight on the floor near his feet, his face hidden in shadow. She gathered herself and walked purposefully across the room to where he was seated.

"James Hatch?" she asked.

The man gestured toward the seat across from him. She sat.

"Father Alan gave me your number?" she said. "I called you …"

He glanced up at her then looked quickly away. His eyes were a shocking bright blue. His face was haggard – puffy and pale, his week's growth of beard flecked with grey. He said nothing, showed no expression.

"My house…," she continued.

His head tipped sideways. He held up his hand to silence her and closed his eyes tightly. His head tilted to the side and he seemed to be listening.

"Father Alan went to the house?" he asked, his eyes opening. Shocking blue. Again, only glancing toward her for a moment.

"He did," she said.

"Did he stay long?"

"No," she replied, gathering her purse against her.

"Perry!" he shouted, raising his finger.

The old man came across the bar with a glass of scotch. He placed it on the table and stood by, waiting.

"Pay him," James said.

Ellen straightened, taken aback. She thought for a moment, then took out a bill and haltingly handed it to the barman. He went away. James took the glass and swallowed half of it.

"It's ten in the morning," Ellen said, her voice going flat.

"What did Father Allen tell you?" James asked, looking away across the room.

"He said you might be able to help. That's all he said," Ellen answered, growing more uncertain with every passing moment.

"It's five hundred dollars," James said. His lips drew back off his teeth and he shuddered. The words came out haltingly. "For me. To come to your house and see what's happening. It's two thousand if I can fix your problem. Maybe more," he finished. "It depends on what's going on."

James continued to avoid direct eye contact. This would have given him a shifty, deceptive quality but for the grief that was written plainly on his face. It was a grief Ellen had seen many times in clients who had experienced catastrophic trauma: in veterans, rape survivors and so many others. It gave her pause, looking at him. She glanced about the room. It was the kind of place she had only been in once or twice as an adult. His low voice was muted by the palpable exhaustion that lingered in the place.

"Why did Father Alan send me to you? What do you do, exactly?" she said.

James began to fidget in his seat. His expression drifted toward something more threatening.

"Did you bring me something personal?" he asked.

"I did," Ellen replied. She slowly drew her father's rosary from her purse. He gestured with his hand, impatient. She considered the rosary for a moment and attempted to hand it to him, but he pulled away, pointing to the tabletop. She lowered it onto the table. He prodded it, using a pen he took from his pocket, moving the beads about.

James closed his eyes again, sitting back. "Someone's digging? You're doing foundation work, something like that?" he asked.

"No," she said.

"Sewer line?" he asked.

"No, nothing. I told you. We're not digging," she said.

He opened his eyes and shook his head, gesturing for her to take back the rosary beads, "Someone's digging,"

Ellen took the rosary and lowered it into her purse.

"So?" she asked.

He took a piece of paper from his pocket and pushed it towards her, along with the ballpoint pen. "Write your address here," he said.

Again she paused.

She thought of Father Alan. He had entered the house with the kindly, practiced smile of his profession. He had left the house, his eyes wide, slowly backing toward the door. Later, he had called, his voice a whisper, "He might be able to help you ..."

"You want me to have a look, put the money on the table," James said.

Ellen studied him for a moment. Every possible red flag was plainly evident. *He might be able to help you.* She took an envelope from her purse and slid it across the table. Taking out her business card, she wrote her address on the back and placed it on top of the envelope.

"I'll have a look in the morning," he said, taking her card and examining it. He read the address and turned it over.

It read Ellen Perry, psychologist.

James sat back, looking at a variety of points around the room, faster and faster. "You're a psychologist," he said, growing openly anxious.

"What's wrong with psychologists?" she asked.

"What's right with them?" he replied, an ugly edge coming into his voice.

Great. I gave him my address, Ellen thought. She reached quickly for the card in his hand. Her fingers bumped his. There was a pulsing in the air. A dimming down of sound and light. His lips pulled back off his teeth. For the first time since she had arrived, he looked her full on in the eyes. Again the startling blue. He began gasping, his entire body abruptly pinned against the back of the booth.

James was plunged into absolute darkness. Instinctively, he felt for his watch on his wrist, to see the glow of the dial, as he did when waking from nightmares. What he felt there was something different. He tried to sit up and could not. Something held him down. He was supremely puzzled. Voices were all around him in the darkness. Cries, whimpering. And the smell of decay, human waste. Something else. A pitching underneath him. *Like the slow turn of a realization.* A massive, rhythmic motion.

Someone was breathing in the absolute darkness next to him. Or failing to breathe. It was the low, wet struggle to move air past too much fluid. Drowning on dry land? He felt out with his hand, found a small arm was next to his. A small hand took his in a fierce grip.

Abruptly, he was back in the bar sitting across from Ellen. He scrambled to his feet, backing away from her, and headed for the exit. Then, through sheer force of will, he turned and came back halfway across the bar.

"You're not safe. Get out of the house," he barked and fled the bar.

James burst out into the afternoon sun.

Why didn't I see it coming? he thought.

With open hands, he slapped his head, the blows falling over and over, as if warding off a swarm of bees. A moan rising, he turned down the alley alongside the bar, kicking up garbage at his feet. He leaned face forward up against the alley wall and braced himself. A long column of vomit erupted from him. He bent wide out from the wall, the vomit splashing toward his shoes. The liquor burned his throat, flooding his nose and eyes: hot, bitter, like dying.

He cried out, more lurching up from within him. He switched to one arm supporting himself and used his free hand to batter his head. He attempted to break away and head down the alley but was forced back to the wall. His cries became inhuman, interspaced with ugly, heaving vomiting.

Again he tried moving, blindly. His skin was awash in pinpoints of white-hot pain, coming in waves across him, like cigarette burns, clutching at him, clinging. *Get off!* He stumbled again and fell into a pile of garbage bags, heaped up, torn open. The black plastic was hot against his face, shutting off his breath, flies circling in the afternoon sunlight. He intentionally let the plastic garbage bag suffocate him, sucking the dirty black plastic into his open mouth, his body's suffocation panic shunting aside the voices crying in his ears, the shock, the loss, the infinite despair, and agony, intermingled with rage.

Behind him at the head of the alley, Ellen stood, aghast. Her purse hung from her hand, swinging slowly, a stately pendulum in stark contrast to the chaos thrashing before her. She stepped forward haltingly and then back again, fearful. With a shock of recognition she saw herself, flinging her body against the bathroom door.

James rose and stumbled away down the alley, falling, and rising, crying out, his voice a ragged hammer blow echoing down the alley. Then he turned and was gone, a single empty soda can rolling slowly to a halt.

Chapter 4

Ellen stepped off the bus and walked the half-block to her house. She was angry with herself and with Father Alan. *What have I opened myself up to?* She practiced the conversation in her head. *I'm sorry Mr. Hatch but I don't think this will work for me. Yes, keep the payment, I don't need it back.*

She saw herself blocking his calls, looking over her shoulder at night. Her fears lurched up, jump-scare fast. The horror of what was happening in her home was no longer contained there. Like a contagion, its impact had spread out to the streets around her, the barrier between what was real and unreal collapsing further.

She opened the low, ornamental metal gate of her yard. Pedestrians pressed past on the narrow sidewalk. She smiled reflexively, ducking her head as they passed. *Can they see how messed up I am?* She stepped through the gate, closing it behind her, already exhausted at the prospect of going into the house. On the porch she saw a large grey cat.

"Olive!" she said. She rushed up the steps and knelt before the grey cat. "Oh, where have you been, sweetie?" She sat on the top step and gathered the cat into her lap. The cat had been missing for weeks, one day suddenly gone. Ellen petted the cat as it turned its face upward to her, eyes closed, purring.

"Somebody's been feeding you, thank god," Ellen said. She

put her face down into the cat's fur, smelling her familiar scent. She let her anxious exhaustion seep into the animal. For a moment, the world fell away, and she was just with. *With.* Not alone. But the moment passed, and the weight of what waited in the house again bore down on her. She turned and looked at the door. Gathering the cat, she rose to enter.

As Ellen approached the door, the cat's ears flattened back, her low growl rising.

"Olive?" Ellen said.

The cat wrenched violently in her arms, twisting to get free. Ellen gripped the cat more firmly as she raised her key to unlock the door. The cat raked her claws along Ellen's hand, and Ellen dropped her. The cat bounded down the steps, ran along the walkway, passed easily between the bars of the ornamental gate; and turning left, raced away down the busy sidewalk.

"Olive!" Ellen shouted. She dropped her things and chased after the cat, which darted left again at the end of the block past the corner deli next door. Reaching the corner, Ellen saw the cat turn left again down the narrow pathway that ran between the deli and a big Victorian home beyond.

Ellen followed the cat down the pathway to the Victorian's back yard and then drew up short. Olive had already disappeared somewhere beyond the yard. To her left, across the small square yard of the corner deli, she could see the back of her own house. Before her, the yard of the Victorian house adjoined her own at its back corner. The yard in front of her was dug up; the product of a new sewer line which required a deep trench bisecting the yard at an angle running partway toward her own yard. The dirt covering the filled in trench was still fresh, grass only beginning to sprout.

Ellen stood at the top of the basement stairs. She held a basket of laundry. The side of her finger hovered beneath the light switch just inside the doorway at the top of the stairs. Below, the darkness offered a kind of blissful not knowing. The light from behind her picked out a few details on the stairs. She could hear the afternoon traffic outside, distant, muted. It called to her. Put the laundry down. Leave.

She pictured the space below. First comes the light switch for the basement. Then, down the stairs. Then, twenty paces along the length of the wall to the washing machine. A minute to load. The sound of the machine starting. Slowly, and with restraint, walking the twenty steps back, turning to look upward at the doorway above. Pausing, intentionally looking across the basement.

Don't rush me. Don't you ever rush me. Not ever.

She flicked the light switch and the bulb at the bottom of the steps came on. She took the first step down, then the second, intentionally pacing her measured steps versus surrendering to the fear. She took each tread with confidence. When she reached the bottom, she raised her hand for the next switch mounted on the post next to her. She reached slowly. Intentionally making the gesture languid. Click.

She turned and looked across the expanse of the basement. Her father's worktables and tools were there. The card table folded against the wall from the good days, when he would deal the cards out to the men who came on summer nights, the garage door swung high and open at the far end; soda cans standing like sentries over the cards. Scores and voices rising and falling; syncopated patterns of behavior. The chips tossed with a flourish into the central pile, clattering lightly. The humor. What one did. What one failed to do. The surprise. The resignation. The commonly held understandings of what was right and fair in life and what was not. The comforting context of those long-gone summer nights.

When Ellen had come into the house it upended the place. When she came, her father, a widower at 42, living in a simple daily rhythm of work and Alcoholics Anonymous meetings, saw her as the making of amends for his drinking and the destruction it had created. For him, the surprise of a child he did not know he had only made the making of amends that much more iconic. He took it on like he took on any other task associated with his sobriety, drawing on the commonly held rules for living that his twelve-step world held as understood. For Ellen's father, remade by his higher power, it was about proof, that we are what we say we will do. And in doing what we say we will do, we are redeemed.

He had met Ellen's mother in a bar. Drank with her. Slept with her. Like many of the people he knew when drinking, the relationship had fallen apart. He had moved on to a new bar, new arguments. His wife of eight years, newly buried in consecrated earth, had left him with a fierce self-loathing. That all he had made was not enough to keep her from leaving him. So, he was committed to making a dead thing out of his rage and confusion; to put it to sleep.

He had felt surprisingly little grief at his wife's death. She was the victim of an illness. He had watched the changes creep up on her, first slowly, then in a cascade until the place where there was once warmth grew cold. You can put your hand there and feel the last patch of heat.

It was his lack of grief that goaded him. For days and then weeks, he waited for it. Like a man at a crossroads awaiting a storm, but instead, the breeze. The gentle movement of grass.

He took up the bottle to end the waiting, but what he found surprised him further, at least for a little while. The bottle made him angry, but it never made him grieve. In fact, in retrospect, it stole that from him. One evening, propped up on his elbow, seeing the amber oily glass before him slip into double, he realized this. It was like watching himself from a distance stepping off a pier into deep water. He knew the bottle had taken his grief and given him nothing in return. After that, there was just the flurry of nothing, over and over.

Fighting or not fighting. Angry or not angry, his wife drifted away, never grieved for. Her dresses and her shoes, the paint she chose for the kitchen. She became flat, like a paper doll cut out from a children's book. He eventually only remembered her from photos. He rose each day to go to his job, then clocking out, to the bars, a functional alcoholic, the grim rhythms unbroken until the day he knew had to choose between dying and going to an AA meeting.

Ultimately, Ellen came to her father's house, years after he had given up the bottle. As he sat at the card table, his index finger and thumb lifting the queen of hearts to discard, she was there, standing in the driveway, her bag beside her; a case worker next to her, frowning down at them all.

Ellen turned past the end of the stairs and walked toward the washing machine, the image of her father at the card table there as she passed. For a moment, she considered opening the garage door and letting out the stale air. The urge passed. She had spent too long keeping what was happening secret.

She opened the washer and put the clothes in. Measured step

by measured step, she added the detergent, plastic blue. Closing the lid with a confident bang. Timer knob turning with a rattle. The machine sprang to life. She put the basket on the dryer and turned to go.

And there she was. At the back of the basement. Standing. A girl in silhouette. Her hair a wild mass. Young, maybe six years old. Naked. A chill rolled across the room. Whispering.

The washer lurched violently next to her. Still filling with water, it rose half a foot and fell with a bang. Ellen leapt backwards. She looked back down the basement, and the girl was gone. The washer lurched again, the sound booming off the basement walls, its side warping from the impact.

Bang again. Ellen backed across the basement and reaching the stairs, walked back up. She reached the kitchen and closed the door. She took out her phone and dialed a number. The call went to voice mail.

"I was wrong," she said. "There's been digging."

Chapter 5

James' pants and coat were twisted about him, his legs dangling off the side of the mattress. He raised his head and looked down at his shoes, stained with vomit.

"Oh, man," he muttered, his head falling back. He reached for the plastic bottle of scotch next to him, drinking down the last of it.

He pushed himself partially upright, struggling to rise on one arm, his head reeling. The motion caused the half-gallon, plastic scotch bottle to roll off the bed and onto the floor with a clatter. He closed his eyes, turned his head, and glanced at the clock by the bed. Eight p.m.

Then he remembered the alleyway, the mad pressure in his head. He struggled upright. His head tipped sideways. He looked again at the empty bottle.

Too much for one afternoon.

You might as well put a gun to your head, he heard a doctor saying. *Alcohol poisoning is a very real possibility.*

He glanced up at the wall covered in taped-up pieces of paper. Biblical pages, pages from the Koran, symbols from Hinduism, Judaism, other faiths. To challenge demons, to invite exorcisms. Religious tokens tacked up. Pictures of movie stars, sports stars. (They help sometimes.) Obituaries. (More help to call on.)

James took a deep, shuddering breath. His body began to shake, a sudden pressure swarming in his head. Shadows began to crowd into the room about him. A fly landed on his cheek. He raised a hand to shoo it away before noticing more of them on the wall. The tabletop next to the bed was now swarming with flies. Three on his hand. Now twenty. Now thousands. The buzzing in the room rose.

James rose to his feet, drunkenly pitching side to side. He stuffed his phone and other items into his pockets. He lunged for the door and half fell down the narrow stairway. Flies swarmed in the dim light of a single bulb below. There was a suffocating smell of things rotten, human waste; the flies raising a terrible humming in the narrow landing before the door. James struggled to breathe, flies crowding around his nostrils and into his mouth. His hand found the doorknob though a mass of insects and he burst though, falling headlong into the darkened alleyway.

"Son of a bitch!" he said, staring back at the empty stairwell.

Hands shaking, he dragged out his phone and flipped though the voicemails until he found Ellen's recent message.

"Nope," he said his voice slurring. He swiped the voicemail sideways, his thumb hovering over the delete button as if deleting the message would somehow undo what had been set in motion.

Then he recalled the darkness. The small fierce hand in his. The low, wet struggle to move air past too much fluid. *A pitching underneath him. Like the slow turn of a realization.* He put his head down and waited for the drunken reeling to lessen. "Fuck," he whispered.

He dialed the number instead.

22

Chapter 6

Ellen sat in the kitchen, waiting for James to arrive. She held a cigarette, noticing that the rising smoke had a ripple in it. Her hand was shaking.

This place is a trap, she thought. She wore a thick sweatshirt and blue jeans with a brown belt. For no clear reason, she had put on her hiking boots. But of course, she had a reason. To be able to kick, fight if she needed to.

It had been months since her father died. She steeled herself for someone to be entering the house for only the second time since his passing. Only one other person had been in the house since two men had taken her father's body out the front door on a wheeled gurney, zipped up in a grey vinyl bag, a funeral home's ornate logo stitched on the side. The first to visit since then had been Father Allen. He had not stayed long. She smiled ruefully.

She thought of the relative calm that had descended for a few days on her father's passing. The complex mix of grief and relief that comes after long-term hospice care ends, a person dies. The hovering sense of immense meaning, impossible to grasp. And the guilt. Thoughts she'd had on the long nights of his relentless suffering. *I wish this would end. What possible meaning can such suffering give him?*

And when the last day came, it was well after midnight, after days of being unconscious. Her father's breathing had become a growling sound. Drops of morphine for the pain. Then an hour later, more drops and the growling stopped. Was it pain? Or was he fighting? A last battle after a life of battles?

Returning after just minutes in the kitchen to get a cup of coffee, she realized with a small moment of surprise that he had gone. "They often leave when we are out of the room," the hospice worker had said. Also, "Don't worry if he doesn't talk to you. He's doing his work. Getting ready to go," she had said. He certainly didn't talk. That much was true.

Her father died and the hospice workers, Carrie, Adam, and Eunice, who had come to help during the long days simply disappeared. Having gone on to other rooms, other unknowably complex cycles of dying; fretting families to be counseled, beds to be cleaned, medicine administered, shame to be calmed, their peaceful measured presence only fully comprehended once gone. There was also sadness there, that her and their shared purpose of measuring and interceding, of acknowledging her father's suffering, of accompanying him in his dying was, in a moment, completed, done. And just like that there were no longer these intimate witnesses to the last months of her life. Nor anyone to witness what came next.

After his passing came a day of peaceful quiet. Was it three? And then the sounds began, coming first in the night. Doors opening on plaintive hinges when they should not have been moving at all. The TV coming on. How at first she had tried to rationalize, to deny each little event. Unplugging the TV. Locking doors. *Maybe if I had left the day he died. Not come back. Sold the house.*

And now, after months of her lonely vigil amidst increasingly impossible madness uncoiling, someone else was going to enter the house. A stranger, apparently an alcoholic. *A dangerous one?*

Her father had put a deadbolt on the inside of her bedroom door for precisely this reason. Because a drunk isn't safe to be around. The moment he did it created far more harm than the seemingly mild event that preceded it. A day before he had lapsed back into drinking. The only time in his years of sobriety she saw him take to drink. It was morning. She was fifteen, standing in the doorway of the bathroom again with a toothbrush in her hand. He was standing at the top of the stairs, weaving side to side, staring at her, such despair in his eyes. After a long few moments, he had turned and walked slowly down the stairs and out the front door, closing it quietly. He was gone until the following day. What had passed through his mind in those moments, she would never know. But nothing was ever the same between them after that. A pall of self-loathing filling the man, driving him to a rigid performance of self-control that stripped him of what little warmth, kindness, and connection he had ever had.

And now here she was, pinning her hopes on a drunk amidst her own crumbling sense of self-control, of sanity. The irony was not lost on her. A garbage bag on the floor brimmed with take-out containers and the refuse of a dozen ashtrays. Dishes were piled in the sink. It was as far as she had gotten cleaning up. It was all she could do to steel herself for this *visit.* She looked at her watch. Ten o'clock, he had said in his message, only an hour away.

There was a loud knock at the door. She jerked upright. Was it the basement door? No. The front door. He was early? She felt anger rising in her. Why early? Why would he do that? She found herself striding down the hall towards the front door. She opened it.

Two police officers stood on the porch.

"Sorry to disturb you, ma'am. May we speak with you?" the female officer asked. She held a notebook.

"Of course," Ellen said. She stepped out onto the porch pulling the door closed behind her. She saw other cops were walking the street, knocking on doors.

"Ma'am, there was an assault on one of your neighbors up the street here last night. The Singhs," the officer continued. She watched Ellen's expression carefully. Instinctively, Ellen shifted into her therapist self, shutting off all visible reactions, creating a demeanor of calm interest.

"They were assaulted in their home," the officer said.

"That's terrible," Ellen replied. She allowed her eyes to show a little alarm, some concern.

"Were you home last night?" the officer asked. The male officer stood a step behind her and to one side. He remained silent.

"Yes, I was. All evening," Ellen said.

"Did you hear or see anything unusual?"

"I'm sorry, I didn't."

"And your name, please?"

"Ellen Giffords."

"This is your home?"

"Yes," Ellen replied.

"Do you know the Singhs?" the officer asked.

"No, I'm sorry I've only been here for a year or so and I really haven't ..." Ellen shrugged.

"Okay," the officer replied making note on her pad.

"Was it a robbery," Ellen asked?

The cop glanced at her partner. "No," she said. "Nothing was taken. Indications are it may have been racially motivated. We'll know more once an investigation is complete."

"Was it bad?" Ellen asked.

"Do you live here alone?" the officer asked.

"Yes, I do," Ellen replied.

The officer handed her a business card.

"Keep your doors locked, the assailants may have been passing through or they may still be in the area. Call us if anything occurs to you that might help us find out who did this."

"Yes, I will. Thank you," Ellen replied.

Racially motivated. Ellen stood for a moment as the two officers descended the porch and exited the yard. For the thousandth time she was taken by the degree to which people made assumptions about her, granted her certain status, made space for her based on how she looked, the way she presented herself. It was a curious thing.

She looked up the block to where two police cars were parked in front of a house, then she turned and went inside.

At ten a.m. Ellen's phone rang.

"I'm a block down, at the noodle shop," James said and hung up.

Chapter 7

Ellen took a small amount of comfort in meeting James away from the house, but her feeling of alarm was jangling. She crossed the street and walked down the block to the small take-out noodle shop. It was one of those with a few stools along one wall for those who wanted to eat in. It was not designed to be comfortable.

She entered to find him at one of the stools eating noodles. She approached him and sat, leaving a stool between them. It was early. They were alone. Most of the staff was in the back preparing for the lunch hour.

"That's the place?" he said, gesturing out the front window down the block toward her house.

She noted the use of "the" instead of "your." It offered her the smallest bit of emotional distance.

"Yes," she said.

"Quiet today?" he asked, tipping the bowl up to drink the last of the soup.

"Are you sober?" she asked him.

He paused for a moment, reflecting on the details at the bottom of his bowl.

"I am," he replied. "But you're making me rethink that choice."

"You scared the hell out of me," Ellen said.

"That's on you," he said, setting his bowl on the small shelf next to him. He continued to avert his eyes. His response made her angry. It was the opposite of an apology. Her anger made her decision easy.

"Mr. Hatch. I'm not sure this is going to work out," she said. The words came out slowly, carefully.

"Well, unfortunately for us both, now you're stuck with me," he replied.

Ellen stood abruptly. "I most certainly am not," she replied. An old man behind the counter looked up for a moment and then went back to his work.

James took a breath and collected himself. "You have the single biggest problem that I have ever encountered, and I've seen some big problems in my day," he said.

"Whatever you say," she said stepping back.

"Your house must be a goddamn circus," he said, his voice lowering. "I spoke to Father Allen. He scares pretty easy, but this time? He's plenty scared. And *you,* you've been in that situation for *weeks*," he said. His jaw worked uncomfortably after he fell silent.

Ellen paused. Resisting the part of her ready to walk away.

"This has every marker of some kind of confidence game," she said. "But Father Allen gave me your name, so I'll give you five minutes to explain to me exactly how you'll be helpful. But no more threats. Do you understand?"

James sighed. "Confidence game. Okay, let's talk about how this confidence game works. We start with a simple yes or no question. Do you have dead people in your house? You know, hanging around? Rattling the pots and pans. Being a pain?" He continued to glance about the shop as he spoke, looking more or

30

less anywhere she was not.

She studied him, her eyes narrowing.

"Moment of truth," he said looking down at his hands, smiling past stained teeth.

"What if I do?" she answered, still standing a few feet away from him.

"Father Allen isn't the only guy who sends people to me. You'd probably know a few of the names. Big houses. Older houses. Anyway, sometimes dead people won't go. Usually anger or grief or some unfinished business keeping them from going. Usually, the scale of the problem is minor. Sometimes it's not. Your problem is not minor."

"Don't play me," she said, anger flickering across her features.

"Why do you say that?" he asked.

"Because I haven't told you a single thing about my problem."

"Oh, you've done more than that," James said. With that he looked directly at her. His bright blue eyes were bloodshot from lack of sleep. The sounds from the restaurant kitchen became muted. A hum rose. Shadows spilled across the walls and floor. Faint shapes moving in and out.

"You brought your problem with you," he said. He looked away and the light from the street again flooded the room, the sounds from the bustling kitchen returned. The shadows were gone.

Ellen slowly went back to her stool. "This is what I've been seeing," she said quietly. She was fighting to maintain her sense of self-control. Her therapist self was quickly giving way to other sides of her nature. Which self was rising? *Too many at once to track.* The side that focused exclusively on self-protection was loud and clear. The skeptic, the side of her desperate to discredit anything, including the months-long evidence of her own ears and eyes. And something else. The expansive side of her. There in the mix of fear, denial and panic was a side of her that was deeply curious. She leaned into that small voice.

"This is from the house?" she asked.

"You brought it with you," he said, looking down.

"Me, it's around me?" she asked.

"It's the biggest mob I've seen attached to anyone, by far," James replied. His body language shifted. He seemed to be suddenly resigned to something. *To not being believed, understood?* She had seen it many times in therapy. The client reaching a plateau, believing they were alone in their experience of the world no matter who they try to explain it to. It was common to those who had experienced traumatic events long ago. That the experience was impossible for they themselves to comprehend, the shock of it trailing back across years, even decades of contradictory layers of meaning making. Meaning sometimes first made as a child.

Ellen kept flickering back and forth between self-protective anger at him, *liar,* and drowning in her own experiences of the last two months. What would years in the house be like? Decades? Panic rose. I have to get out of this before it goes on too long. She stood. *Walk away from him,* a voice inside her said. Immediately the reply came. *And then go to what's waiting in the house.* Trapped.

Ellen realized he was not just resigned. He was also waiting. He noticed her looking at him and smiled, continuing to avert his gaze.

"We have one more step," he said.

"What?" she replied. Her curious side was continuing to rise to the forefront, gaining a foothold.

"The part where you make the crazy person prove to you that you're not crazy," he replied.

"Okay," Ellen said, "So prove it."

He glanced up at her. "We'll that's refreshingly direct."

"Prove I'm not crazy," she said laughing ruefully. "I can certainly see the value of that."

Chapter 8

Ellen opened the gate to the yard and James followed her in. He looked up at the tall narrow Edwardian home.

"This yours?" he asked.

"It was my father's," she replied.

James walked along the side of the house to the back yard, took a brief look and then came back. He began to climb the stairs and stumbled.

"Are you all right, James?" she asked.

"Call me Jimmy," he responded, not looking back.

Ellen walked up the steps and unlocked the front door. She pushed it open. After a moment, James entered the house. He walked to the middle of the entry hall and halted. She heard him grunt, then breath whistled out between his teeth. Not looking back, he held out his hand towards her, palm flat, signaling for her to wait. She stepped in, closed the front door, and waited.

He climbed the stairs that lead up to the second floor. His footfalls were sluggish on the creaking stairs, like a person carrying a great weight. The house was silent. A car honked out on the street, muted, a world away.

Ellen stood by the door, feeling like a stranger in the house, as if she had ever felt any other way. Her anxiety rose. She knew what this velvet-thick silence meant. That it preceded activity.

Entering the house alone for the past two months had been

crushing; the full weight of it unknown to her until this moment. The thought of this man being her sole alternative to going back to that, to being here alone, brought up lurching panic. She realized with a shock that she was already clinging to the idea that this battered man could help her, even as she legitimately feared he might harm her.

She had worked with domestic violence perpetrators as part of her counseling internships. They had taught her fundamental lessons on what it means to be trapped by a man. They had taught her just how quickly the thin veneer of civility, even in the therapy room, could shatter. She had only ever called for security once. A man's lip curling up to reveal a snarl, teeth, his feral need to lash out in a lifetime of lashing out.

Trapped.

She had studied, learned, worked to build a successful career as a therapist. Her completion of a PhD in counseling had been driven by her passion for learning, yes, most certainly, but close behind that was financial security, independence; a career that insured she could insulate herself, keep herself safe. She had understood from an early age that it was up to her to avoid being trapped by circumstances, by bad decisions, by controlling men. That priority had informed a lifetime of her decisions. Including remaining single.

At times, bullying men had entered her orbit, puffed up with their own importance, smelling of appetite and anger and behind that, fear. Men whose self-validation came at the expense of others, of women most of all. Employers, professors, leading voices in her field, all expecting her to acquiesce to, to seek proximity to their positions, their presumptions of power, their intellectual certitude. She had not. With the most subtle performances of opaque courtesy she had moved past them, circumvented them, declined their hinting demands. Obscuring herself in a seemingly impenetrable combination of sexual naivete and ambiguity, she had become invisible, avoided the traps that had trapped so many other women.

She had maintained her hard-earned autonomy up until her father fell ill, his aging body turning on him step by step. He was diagnosed with amyotrophic lateral sclerosis, ALS, his nervous system slowly breaking down. Initially, she tried to maintain her carefully guarded independence; a professional woman managing her practice, busy, industrious. But avoiding his illness and the brutal suffering she knew it would eventually cause him was more than she could live with. In her carefully protected life, a life with no husband, no children, it felt like one careful choice too many, that if she ignored his illness, it would remain something forever done badly, done like he might have done.

Reluctantly, she had returned to live in the house. Leaving him with the hospice caretakers during the days, returning to care for him over the long nights. But despite their proximity, no deeper conversations took place. No stories emerged of the past, of her childhood, of her mother. Not his history. No final embellishments of his faltering story. And so, it came down to the simplest of relationships; her feeding him when his motor control was too far gone to raise a spoon to his lips, her changing his bedsheets while he remained in place, her cleaning him like an infant.

In sacrificing her freedom, nothing had emerged, no greater understanding, no resolutions, regrets, apologies, grand final gestures; no further meaning or connection than she had with him as a child. She had resigned herself to caring for him, his stoic silence hanging over the house, balancing itself against her own.

As the final months came and went, she understood the degree to which growing up in his house had been the formative engine of her life. Coming back and experiencing his stoic silence as an adult, as a woman with a vast range of capacities for helping others express, reinforced for her an awareness of the part of herself that was not so different now from him.

Following his death, having passed first through his living, breathing isolation, she had passed through deeper veils, dying, death, now haunted by a vast anger which had suddenly blossomed only after he died. She was ready to give herself up to it. To the vast inertia of this stoic anger. To sit amongst the whispers and be lost.

But then James stepped through the door and the terrible inertia shifted. Like an earthquake, what was presumed to never move was moving. In an instant, she knew she would not be able to return to that terrible isolation. This man, stepping across the threshold had ended her dull, grieving resentments, her seeming surrender to the frozenness of her father's empty house.

At his arrival, she was seeing things that she had not seen before. Things now continually visible out of the corner of her eye, shadows that swirled around him. But not only him, also her. Shadows moving between her and even her own hands, raised and open in front of her.

She heard Jimmy's slow footsteps in the upstairs hall. She heard the one particular door to her father's room open, the way the doorknob rattled, the short squeak of the hinge at the beginning of the door's slow arc.

Well, he's in it now, she thought.

Chapter 9

James was struggling to breathe in the long hallway. He paused before the first door, his chest heaving. He felt sweat dripping along his ribs, the acrid smell of fear rising. He placed his fingertips on the door to the bedroom. He pushed it slowly open. The room was awash in sunlight. On a hospital bed, stripped of sheets, its plastic mattress yellowed by years of use, an old man sat, his body wasted away. He looked up, his eyes white with cataracts. He slowly shook his head *no.* James stepped back as the door drifted closed.

Christ, I should have seen it coming, he thought. He turned, steadying himself against the wall as waves of dizziness swarmed over him. He wiped his face and started back towards the stairs to descend.

Something was drawing his attention to the kitchen. He reached the bottom the stairs and raised a finger to his lips. Ellen was standing where he had told her to wait. *Something's wrong,* he thought, shaking his head for her to see. He raised his hand again to signal her to stay.

A great suffocating weight was on the house, far out of scale for one old man sitting on one old, pissed-on hospital bed. James squared his shoulders and walked down the hall to the kitchen at the rear of the house. He felt the inevitability of what was coming next. A certain grim determination settled over him. The kitchen too was flooded with light. He saw the full trash bag teetering to one side amidst the riot of disarray. There was the smell of stale cigarette smoke. He saw the couch in the nook, realizing how many weeks she had been sitting there. He looked back along the hall to where Ellen stood half visible by the door. He held up his hand, signaling her to wait yet again.

He turned beyond her line of sight and something under the floor beneath his feet, something vast, pulled him to the door leading to the basement. There was a flashlight on the floor next to the door. He turned it on and opened the door.

He set his foot on the stairs. Next to him was a light switch. He switched it on. A lightbulb illuminated the bottom of the stairs. The basement extended beyond his line of sight both ways. He began to descend. His breaths came in short gasps, his eyes glowing fierce blue in the dim light. As he reached the bottom of the stairs, he pointed the flashlight to the shadowy recesses in the back of the basement. He heard something, whispering. He cocked his head sideways. So many voices.

When James began screaming, it shattered the silence, along with something else, a deep booming coming from below. Ellen bolted down the hallway to the kitchen, turning the corner to the basement door. It was closed. She yanked on the doorknob violently. The door would not open. Somewhere below Jimmy was screaming, the same high-pitched ragged scream she had heard him make in the alley that day. The booming below her feet was matched by the perfect high-pitched ringing of two glasses on the kitchen counter as they rattled against each other. Other items, spoons, forks, a lighter, paper clips, pens, hopped about with each concussion. Ellen glanced frantically about the room. She bolted to the storage closet. Canned foods and dry goods on the higher shelves, tools on the lowest. She grabbed a pry bar, ran back to the basement door, and jammed it into the gap between the doorknob and the door frame. Wrenching violently, she tore the door open, splintering the frame.

James had stopped screaming. But the booming was growing louder, more insistent. She took the stairs two at a time, landing on her feet at the bottom. Toward the back of the basement, a flashlight lay on the cement floor, its beam illuminating the side of Jimmy's body where he lay collapsed on the floor.

The booming was so very deep. She felt its impact in her gut and lungs. It threatened to take over the rhythms of her breathing, her heart. She dropped to one knee next to Jimmy. He was convulsing, his eyes rolling back in his head. Red vomit spilled down his cheek and out across the floor. He had bitten his tongue. Ellen put her hand on his shoulder, preparing to turn him onto his back. She glanced up towards the back of the basement. There in the shadows she saw a figure standing. The silhouette of a man with a strange deformity. At first Ellen thought the man had too many elbows. Then she realized what she was seeing. Multiple compound fractures.

"Oh, fuck this," she said. She took Jimmy's hands together and pulled him to an upright position. Taking him around his chest, she yanked him up to a nearly standing position. Then, throwing her shoulder low, she lifted him into a fireman's carry.

Ignoring the back of the basement, ignoring the sound, ignoring the terrible form of the man where there should be none, she staggered towards the stairs. The booming was an awful, angry roaring. She gritted her teeth and climbed, sure that one of the steps was going to break under her, sending them both back down.

But the stairs held, and they fell out onto the floor of the sunlit kitchen. She kicked the remains of the basement door closed and the booming shut off instantly, as if it had never happened at all.

Chapter 10

The Emergency room was a long row of treatment bays. James lay in the bed, an IV in his arm, electronics beeping out his life signs. He continued to remain unconscious after the long ambulance ride, intake, and treatment. Now the scrum of ER doctors had moved on to others, leaving Ellen and James momentarily alone amidst the mad bustle of the ER, the long curtain drawn about them, offering some privacy.

Around midnight, Jimmy moaned and shifted. Not thinking, Ellen put her hand on his arm to calm him. She realized a doctor had entered to stand at the foot of the bed. He held a chart, one page folded back over the top. He was watching James closely. Ellen took note of his nametag, Dr. Dorsa. Was he the attending? After a few moments, Ellen began to speak, but the doctor turned, as if remembering something, and was gone through the narrow gap in the curtain.

Ellen rose to follow him. She passed through the curtain and out into the main room, but he had disappeared. She returned to James' bedside.

A few minutes later, a second doctor swept the curtain back and entered. She walked to the opposite side of the bed and looked down at James.

"Ms. Perry, I'm Doctor Marino" she said. "Are you a family

member?"

"I'm his cousin," Ellen replied.

"Are there any other family members we can contact," the doctor asked.

"No, I'm sorry, there's not. How is he?" Ellen replied.

The doctor looked at her for a moment and made a note. "Mr. Hatch has acute alcohol poisoning." She continued to flip though his chart. "We're getting his fluids up. Does he drink like this regularly?"

"I don't know," she replied.

"Drugs?"

"I'm sorry I don't know," Ellen replied.

The doctor closed the chart. She looked at Ellen, a myriad of questions there, just behind the pause.

"This is not the first time we've seen him. He refuses treatment. He won't accept outpatient treatment for addiction. And then, a few months later, if he's lucky, a year later, he's back again, like clockwork." She paused, "He won't last. If you don't get him some help, he'll drink himself to death."

The doctor gathered herself to go. "We'll discharge him in the morning, assuming he stays that long. Now, if you'll excuse me," she said, turning to go.

"Doctor?" Ellen asked. "Is there a Doctor Dorsa here at the hospital?"

Dr. Marino turned back. "He was here at the hospital a number of years ago. It was before my time," she replied. With that, she left.

Ellen sat again next to James' bed. A brief search on her phone told her what Dr. Marino did not. Dr. Dorsa had indeed worked here. Twenty years ago, he had had a massive heart attack while making rounds in the pediatric ward. They had named the ward after him. Ellen looked up to see a hospital social worker, a look of surprise on her face.

"Ellen?"

"Terry," Ellen said, putting on a bright voice. She gathered herself. Terry was a young therapist at Ellen's practice. She was working towards her PhD, getting clinical hours at the hospital.

"How are you?" Ellen said. She put out her hand.

"Very well, thank you," Terry replied. "I just had a talk with Doctor Marino. She suggested I stop by. I had no idea you were the woman … who was with him," she finished. "We've tried to get Mr. Hatch into treatment. He always refuses. Are you treating him?" she suddenly added.

Dammit, Ellen thought. *This is way too close to home.*

"Oh, no. Not at all. As you know, I'm on leave at the moment," Ellen replied.

"Then what brought you here?" Terry said, her surprise at encountering her senior co-worker and a therapist of no small reputation, causing her professional demeanor to slip.

Over the course of months, the two had formed a growing friendship at the office. Somewhere between a mentor relationship and something more personal. Ellen had come to appreciate Terry's quick, intuitive mind and her astute mindfulness of office relationships, boundaries.

"He's a man from the neighborhood. He wasn't well. There was no one else, so I brought him in," Ellen replied, smiling. She shrugged.

"Doctor Marcasio sent me over on a psych consult," Terry said, lowering her voice.

"For Jimmy?" Ellen asked, immediately regretting the

familiarity of using the name.

Terry gathered herself. "You told her this man is your cousin?" she said, her head turning slightly.

"I lied to her. Look I feel some responsibility for him collapsing. He was doing some work …"

Terry looked at her closely. "Is everything all right?"

Ellen was aware of how she was dressed, how disheveled she looked. She noticed with relief the young woman wasn't taking notes.

"Yes, yes, it's fine. I'll make sure he's taken care of, and I'll head home. No worries," Ellen replied. "I really do appreciate your concern." Ellen used a slight shift in tone to indicate the conversation was ending. "I promise you, I'm fine," she reiterated, adding a touch of warmth.

Terry's phone beeped. She glanced down at it. "Well, that's me. Never a dull moment on the night shift. I'll come back in a couple of hours and check on Mr. Hatch." She handed Ellen her card. "Call me if you need anything at all." She shook Ellen's hand, and she was gone.

Ellen turned to see Jimmy removing his IV, sweat was pouring down his face. He looked manic. Worse.

"You need to lay down, Jimmy," she said, growing increasingly alarmed. She stepped forward, preparing to gently push him back down in the bed.

James put a hand up, and dropping his head, held perfectly still. "I promise you, you absolutely don't want to touch me right now," he said. He began moving again. He expertly poked a few buttons on the monitoring equipment and then removed the sensors on his hand.

"What you're doing is dangerous, Jimmy. You could have

another seizure," Ellen said. She was considering calling a nurse.

"I most certainly could," he replied. "Use your head. Do you have any idea how many people have died in this bed?" he said.

She quickly gathered up her things and followed him out.

Chapter 11

James and Ellen were in a room at a newly built motel a short way up the peninsula. Grand opening, the sign outside had said. James was asleep face down on one of the two beds. He was fully clothed. The sheets were not turned down. The lights were all on. The TV was blaring a 24-hour news channel.

Ellen sat in a chair by the door. She was slowly twirling an unlit cigarette between her fingers, reviewing the series of events that put her with a man she did not know in a hotel room where she didn't feel safe unless she sat directly by the door. As she worked to piece together the timeline, the things she had seen in the basement kept lurching up into her consciousness. The rush to get Jimmy to the hospital had temporarily shunted to one side that experience. Now those memories were surging up.

She was rapidly losing her sense of what was real and what was not. She attempted to focus her mind on reconstructing the timeline. The goal was to list the events, notice patterns of cause and effect, define what was emerging.

But the effort wasn't working. Not remotely. Each time she attempted to order the events in her mind, images would lurch up, and she would collapse back into a closed loop of fear and anger, replaying in her mind what she had witnessed. Her father. The shadows about Jimmy. The figure in the basement. The stink of alcohol running through everything. The silhouette of the man, his arms broken.... She jerked upright and then settled again into the angry stillness of watching her world collapse. She glanced at the blaring TV.

"In the top of the news, San Francisco police have reported another in a rash of race-related hate crimes directed at minority businesses in the historic Embarcadero District. Mayor Nelson is calling this series of violent crimes a blight on the city's long history of racial and social tolerance. Sources in the community say that a long simmering resentment toward the increasing number of minority businesses has resulting in the recent vandalism and beatings."

A young man was being interviewed. "This neighborhood used the be different. You know? Now it's either foreigners buying up everything or homeless people. These homeless guys are everywhere. People here don't want them. Any of them," he said. *What's he smirking about?* she thought.

The news report continued as James woke up.

"What time is it?" he said loudly.

"Do we have to have the TV?" Ellen replied.

James took the remote next to him and muted the TV. "It helps," he said. "What time is it?" he repeated.

"It's well after midnight," Ellen answered.

"I should eat," he said.

The small diner was closed. The blinds were down. An old man had appeared at the door and opened it to let Jimmy and Ellen in, turning the deadbolt behind them.

It wasn't much of a place, a narrow storefront with a few booths down each wall. The ceiling had tin decorative panels common a hundred years before. The floor, red and white linoleum

50

tiles, was worn pale where decades of feet had passed.

James and Ellen sat in a booth mid-way towards the back. They ate food brought from the dimly lit kitchen by the old man. He stayed for the minimum amount of time needed to set the food down and go.

"That guy loves me," Jimmy said, eating like a starved man.

"Why is he here serving us? It's nearly two in the morning," Ellen asked looking down at her plate of eggs.

"He lives in the back, so it's not a long trip for him."

Ellen felt her anger rising again. The small plastic water glass in front of her was the kind she remembered from the diners of her childhood. Her mother would take her to eat at a place down near the Tenderloin, employees shouting out orders, driving the constant call and response of that kind of joint. Abruptly Ellen shook off the image of her mother, drinking a cold beer at nine in the morning.

"Why go to that motel?" she asked James.

"It's new construction. No history," he said.

"Why not just go home?" she asked.

He stopped chewing and looked at her. "When we first met in the bar. When you tried to take back your business card. You touched my hand," he replied.

She recalled the chaos that had instantly resulted. *You're not safe. Get out of the house.* "Okay," she said.

"When you touched me, your really big problem become my really big problem. I can't stay at my place anymore. Apparently, I'm going to be having trouble like that now," he held up his hands.

"That one moment of contact?

"If you touching my hand set this off, I don't know what you hauling me up a flight of stairs will do," he said ruefully. "Did I thank you for dragging me out of your basement? Thank you." He shook his head.

She let his sarcasm pass.

"So, what did you find out?" she asked.

"I found out fuck all," he said, his anger suddenly right there. "If this keeps up though," he said, slapping his head multiple times, "I'm probably going to stroke out." He dropped his fork on the plate, putting his head between his hands.

She looked at him for a long moment. Something about their dynamic felt familiar to her. And, of course, there it was, why she was feeling angry. She had seen it in her clients, how they had made little decisions here and there to cut themselves off bit by bit from within a marriage, from co-workers, as parents and *from* parents. Little choices to let go of parts of relationships because the cost of being present seemed too unfathomable, too painful, too raw, or just too much trouble. Then one day, a crisis hits and there's no one to turn to, they're completely alone.

How ironic that she, a therapist, had gotten this far in her shell of careful self-protection. But for him, for this man in front of her, no other choice but self-isolation had ever been possible. *I have choices.* She felt her view of the situation expand. Her anger retreated. A calmness stole over her.

"Doesn't seem like there's anyone else," she said.

James looked up from between his hands.

"We're going to have to work together," she said.

She could see him turning things over in his mind, his anger there just below the surface.

"Look, normally this is how it goes," he said. "People call me. I show up. I see whatever is there. I get closer. Then I see a light.

Then they see the light. They go. That's it. I don't talk to them. They don't notice me. It's just the light, and then they go," he said.

"They go," she said slowly gesturing.

"Yeah, that's what they normally do," he replied.

"But this time they're not doing that?"

James began laughing. "No, they're not doing that."

"Can we go back to what happened. Step by step. You entered the house and then what happened?" Ellen asked.

James' features grew dark. "You snooping around in my brain doesn't come with the service," he said.

"Be civil. I just want to try to understand what happened," she replied.

His eyes flashed up to meet hers. "What *is happening*," he responded. As his eyes met hers, the room quieted. Shadows moved in a slow arc about them.

This time, she broke eye contact and looked away. "I understand. You don't have to do that," she said.

"You have a lot of nerve," he replied. You show up, blow everything up, and now you think we're going talk this through, maybe do some therapy?" he replied. "You have thoroughly fucked up my life. I had nothing to do with what fucked up yours."

Her anger surged up to meet his.

"This thing we're doing?" She turned back to purposefully look him in the eye. Again, the room irised down to shadows, the sounds muffled. She held his gaze, gesturing to the two of them. "This is not *remotely* therapy. If I was your therapist, which I am not, I'd be referring you out because I'm in no condition to do therapy for anyone. I've been trapped in a nightmare for two months and I am *not* doing well."

"I'm having acute anxiety manifesting as physical pain, deep depression, loss of ability to focus and, if I'm being honest, suicidal ideation, and the only hope I have at the moment is you, which to any objective observer would not look hopeful. But this is where we are. So, no, this is not talk therapy, it's us figuring out how to fix this. So if you could please get on board, I'd appreciate it, because I don't know how much longer I'll be able to keep going," she said.

James pursed his lips. He was flashing back to the dozens of mental health professionals who had treated him in his early years, including the years he had spent in an institution. A place he where might still be, had he not learned to pretend he was better. Had he not learned to say nothing about his world to such people. Ever. Breaking that silence rule now was possible only because she had just done it first, right there in front of him. But the moment of speaking came with no small effort. He drew a long breath. Then another.

"The entry hall and the front room aren't the problem. Upstairs is active, but straightforward. The kitchen is a little weird, but the basement, towards the back, that's the problem," he said. His heart was suddenly racing. He saw the electroshock table they had strapped him to at sixteen years of age. The wooden dowel being forced between his teeth.

Ellen took in what he was saying and the distress it created for him. Intuitively, she spoke. "My father died in the house two months ago after a long illness. I was taking care of him for nearly a year," she paused. There was a moment of hesitation. She was trying the words in her head before saying them. "I see him now. Upstairs. Also in the kitchen. On the stairs to the basement," she said.

He was looking at her. *Trading me. One for one,* he thought.

He continued. "I told you to wait. I went upstairs. I saw your father. He was there, sitting on a hospital bed of some kind? An old man. He had cataracts," he said.

"He's there," Ellen said. Tears began to spill down her face. She angrily wiped them away. "Why?"

"He did something odd. Something I haven't seen in a long time," James continued. "He looked at me, nodded his head, no."

Ellen sat back, still wiping away tears.

"I have no idea what he meant," Jimmy replied. "But they don't do that. Not normally."

"What's changed?" Ellen asked.

James suddenly sat back, reappraising her. "Someone told me a long time ago that if two people have the sight, it becomes stronger. They amplify it in each other," he said.

"Are you talking about me?" Ellen said.

"I came back down the stairs. I passed you again right before I walked to the kitchen," James continued. He began to show signs of distress as he continued speaking. "When I get there, I understand its below me, really clearly. So, I go down the stairs to the basement," he continued. "Then, it's like a dam breaking. They're all around me," he said. "…but no light," he whispered. He looked up at Ellen, puzzlement spreading across his face. "I was right there, in the middle of them. There was no light. The light never came.

Chapter 12

By the time they returned to the house it was three a.m. Ellen and James sat in her car, parked nearby. Even with the windows down, she was aware of how badly he smelled, but she remained in the car as the weight of what waited in the house bore down on her.

"Thinking I was having some kind of psychotic break was easier," she said.

"Yeah, good times," James replied. He got out of the car and walked towards the house. She followed him. When they reached the house, he walked up onto the porch first. She joined him and unlocked the door.

"When we're in, stay in the front room," James said. "We'll be okay there."

The door swung open. The hall light was on. They turned left and entered the front room of the house. James turned on the lights and raised a finger to his lips signaling for them to be quiet.

In a low voice, he said, "I'm going to see if the hallway is okay." He started towards the hallway and paused. Then, he returned to sit on the couch gesturing to Ellen to also sit. She took up a seat on the opposite end. James prepared to speak and then again, stopped. He cocked his head to one side and then she heard it too. The whispering. She had never heard it in the front room, only ever in the kitchen.

James' body language shifted. She looked across at him. His eyes were glowing blue. He made a V with his two fingers, pointed to his eyes and then down to the floor. The whispering grew louder.

Ellen looked down at her hands folded in her lap. Her watch, facing up, read 3:16. A shadow fell across the face of the watch. She stole a final peripheral glance sideways to see James, his chin drawn down against his chest, making himself small. Then she did the same and waited for a blow to fall. It never did.

Her watch read 3:49 when the shadow withdrew. It did so without any forewarning. It simply withdrew and was gone. She continued waiting until she heard Jimmy shift his weight. She looked sideways towards him, and their eyes met. He shrugged and raised his head.

"I guess the front room is okay," he said.

She pressed her palms into her eyes. "I'd kill for cigarette," she said. "Of course, they're in the kitchen."

"I need a walk. What do you smoke?" he asked.

She told him.

"I'll be back in a few minutes," he replied. "Stay in the front room." He let himself out. She heard his footfalls descending the stairs. She took her jacket, wadded it up under her head and lay down on the couch.

For a blissful time she dozed. Then she dreamed that someone was screaming. She searched in her dream but could not locate the source. When she woke with a start, she realized the screaming was happening on her front porch.

She rose off the couch, picked up a tall, slender statue from the mantle, and brandishing it like a club, opened the front door. There, blocking the door, stood James, blood pouring down from his nose.

Beyond him was a young man, collapsed, his back jammed up against the railing, kicking his feet in a futile effort to continue backing up. His head was shaved. He was screaming, his eyes wide with terror. He crawled sideways, until he reached the stairs, tumbling backwards down the steps. He rose and ran scrambling to get over the gate and away. A half block or so down the street he finally stopped screaming, his voice fading away. Lights came on the porch across the street, but no one came out to see. After a few more moments, the lights turned off.

James had one hand up, covering his bloody nose.

"What happened?" she asked.

"He's not happy about homeless people," James replied. "Says I'm letting down the white race."

"Jesus," Ellen said. "Come in." She stepped back into the house making room for him to pass.

"I told him he really didn't want to touch me," he said, setting her cigarettes on the hall table.

Chapter 13

Afternoon sunlight flooded the front room. Ellen woke on the couch. James sat across from her in a chair. She started upright, coming out of a dream she couldn't recall. It took a moment for her to get her bearings.

"Did you sleep?" she asked him.

"Yes," he said.

Dried blood covered the front of his shirt and jacket. It was on his hands, making black arcs of his fingernails.

"I need a bath," he said.

She realized he'd likely been sitting there waiting to ask for a while. It was not a huge surprise, but the request made her sick to her stomach. *All my boundaries are collapsing.* It made her angry and, surging up beneath that was fear.

"Give me a couple of minutes. I'll find you something to wear, which I'll will leave in the bathroom. After that, I'm going to the store. Please be done and downstairs by the time I return. I'm also going to leave a plastic bag for your clothes. Please don't leave them in the house," she replied.

He shrugged. "Okay," he said.

Ellen walked to the local grocery a few blocks down. She gathered some items and took them to the front. There were two cash registers. A young Asian man began checking out her items.

To her left, a man put a six pack of canned colas on the counter. An old Asian woman rang them up.

In a corner above them, a TV screen showed the evening news. The announcer said, "Tonight at five, late-breaking news on the racial strife in North Beach. The mayor's office received a bomb threat ..."

The screen went silent. The young man who was checking out her groceries held the remote in his hand.

"It makes my grandmother nervous," he said.

"It makes me nervous," Ellen replied.

"This is $4.79," said the man buying colas.

"$4.99," said the old woman.

"The sign back there says $4.79," the man responded.

"I'm sorry," the old woman said. She smiled broadly pointing to the balance due on the cash register.

"Do you speak English?" the man asked her.

"I'm sorry, $4.99," the old woman repeated, smiling.

"Does anyone here speak fucking English," the man said, his voice suddenly threatening.

The young man helping Ellen paused. "What do you need, sir?" he asked.

"Not a goddamn thing if you don't know what your own prices are," the man barked out.

Ellen spoke to him in a level voice. "Why don't you just go," she said.

The man turned and held Ellen's gaze for a moment, smiling. He swept the cans onto the floor and walked out. Ellen and the young man exchanged shocked glances.

James and Ellen sat a few feet apart on the steps of the porch.

The city filed past, oblivious. The afternoon light slanted in from above the buildings across the way, casting gold across everything. Cars and trucks negotiated the cluttered street just beyond the gate. No words had passed between them since she had returned and joined him on the porch.

Ellen felt her anger boiling at the man in the store. She had seen that smile before in her domestic violence work. It was the smile of an abuser, threatening his target. She also knew her anger toward him was out of scale. *I should not have spoken to him,* she thought. *I'm losing my impulse control.*

She looked at James. He sat with his eyes closed, the sunlight warming his face. He was clean, his hair combed back. He wore a plaid shirt her father had worn for years, and would never wear again. With death, the simplest of observations carry staggering permanence. Not for the last time, Ellen considered her own death. *There's no one ahead of me any longer.*

James was taking slow, deep breaths. She noticed the intentional space he maintained between them, creating separation on the wide steps. She was watching him now, looking for signs of the anger and edginess that had defined her experience of him. Strangely, they were gone. She didn't like it, for all his agitation to have disappeared so completely. True, he was calming himself, but something else was going on. She broke the silence.

"How are you feeling?" she asked.

He opened his eyes. "I feel..." he paused searching for the word. "... relaxed? Look me in the eyes," he said.

Ellen shifted around to look towards him. Her eyes met his. The shadows that normally arose, the quieting down of sounds. Both were absent.

"Before, upstairs I felt something." James said. "But here on the porch. Nothing. I don't have a day of my life where there isn't something." He gestured vaguely about himself. "Beyond the gate there, it gets busy again, but here?" He touched his fingers to his forehead, frowning briefly.

"Is your big problem keeping smaller problems away?" he said, uncertain.

"Is that a good thing?" she asked.

"I read a book on addiction," he replied. "It talked about how when there's a blackout in a city, it's the only time we become aware of the ambient sound that electricity makes all around us. We only realize how loud electricity is when it's gone. He said this is why people become addicted to pain killers after an injury. They take an opiate as pain relief for a physical injury, or surgery, and the pain of their emotional stuff goes away too. Once they feel what it's like for that to be gone, they don't want it to come back." His expression began to shift.

"I'm not sure I like this," he said, all the peace was evaporating from his expression. He turned and looked back toward the street.

"I'm nearly out of cigarettes," she said.

There was a moment's pause. "Okay," he said.

He rose, slowly. He walked down the steps to the gate. She saw him square his shoulders. Then he opened the gate and walked out into the flow of foot traffic.

It was later. Ellen descended the stairs from the second floor, drying her wet hair. She wore blue jeans, hiking boots and a sweater. Since she was young, she had thought of blue jeans as being like armor. Wearing them remained a crucial piece of self-protection for her.

She turned to go towards the front room and paused, listening. Then, steeling herself, she instead walked down the hall towards the kitchen. She arrived in the sunlit room, conscious of how loud her boots sounded on the wooden floors. She stood for a moment and then proceeded on to the couch in the breakfast nook. She bent down, took the half empty pack of cigarettes on the side table, straightened up. *Slowly,* she thought. *Don't let them hurry you.* She turned toward the basement door, its wood frame splintered alongside the doorknob.

She took the broom and swept up the wood splinters and metal parts. It made a huge racket. She scooped it all into a dustpan and dumped it in the big trash bag still sitting on the floor. She returned the broom and dustpan to where they belonged and, taking a bottled drink from the refrigerator, walked with the trash bag back up the hallway and out the front door. Her pace remained slow and measured all the way down the hall.

I will not be rushed. I will not be hurried.

Because she did not look back, she did not see the figure of the young girl standing at the opposite end of the long hallway, silhouetted in the afternoon light.

Chapter 14

"You said there was digging," James barked out from beyond the gate. She looked up from her phone to see him standing there. "Show me." His agitation was clearly back.

She walked down and passed through the gate.

"It's around the corner," she said. "How are you?"

"The world is still the world," he responded.

They turned at the corner deli. Turning again, they walked down the path between the deli and the Victorian house. A woman was standing in the back yard. She turned, a folder in one hand.

"The open house is just about finished for today," she said smiling. She offered them a sales sheet.

"Can we just take a quick peek?" James said.

Ellen glanced toward him. His voice was pitched higher, cheerful. *Okay then,* she thought.

The real estate agent shrugged. "Sure, of course," she said. She pointed across the back yard before them. "New sewer service hooking up to the main city sewer line here," she said.

It was the trench that Ellen had seen before. James strolled out along it. "All the way to the city service?" he asked. Again, the bright voice.

"Yes, three feet deep. These city mains ran every which way in the old days," the woman replied. "Won't need that done again for another fifty years."

James strolled back toward them, and they entered the back door of the towering Victorian.

"It's lovely," Ellen said.

"Complete gut renovation," the real estate agent replied. "And the owners are *very* motivated. Moved the last of their things out this morning."

"Why are they selling?" James asked.

"Some kind of health problems or something," she replied, lowering her voice. She shrugged. "They put a ton of money into the place. Are you acquainted with the neighborhood?" she asked.

"Looking for a little more space," Ellen replied.

"Aren't we all," the saleswoman replied. "Here's my card, by the way, if you're selling, I have a lot of interested buyers."

James walked away from them. He opened the hallway door to the basement. The real estate agent started to follow him.

"These are all new windows?" Ellen asked, strolling the opposite way into the dining room.

"Yes, they are. Is that your husband? He needs to be careful on those stairs," the real estate agent said glancing back toward where James had disappeared.

"Oh? Why is that?" Ellen asked.

"Confidentially, the seller took a terrible fall. The wife," she replied. After giving James a few more moments, Ellen walked back into the hallway.

"How is the basement?" she asked.

"You're going to love it," the real estate agent replied.

Ellen opened the basement door and looked down into the brightly lit area below. "Jimmy?" she said. She descended the stairs, the real estate agent behind her. The basement included a vast range of exercise equipment along one side. James was standing at the other end facing an extravagant wet bar.

"This home gym. Isn't it just to die for?" the real estate agent said.

James turned to face them. Sweat was pouring down his face. "Time to go," he said, as he marched past them to the stairs. Ellen had to pull the real estate agent out of his path. He climbed the stairs two at a time. Ellen quickly followed James as he passed.

"Thank you so much," she called back over her shoulder.

"If I can get your email …" the real estate agent's voice drifted up from behind them.

They emerged into the hall and James walked straight out the back door, turned toward the street alongside the house, and was quickly out on the sidewalk heading away from the house. He did not slow his pace as he turned the corner in front of the deli. There was a bench in front. He sat down heavily.

When Ellen caught up to him, she could see he was in trouble. She sat next to him on the opposite end of the small bench. "What's happening?" she asked.

"They're jammed into the place like sardines in a can. I can't stay long enough to get focused. I can't keep from overloading. I can't …" James was gasping. "I can't … There's no air, I can't …"

A few of the people passing on the street, glanced at them, noticing the man's growing state of agitation. He was staring at nothing. "Oh, god," he said, his voice rising.

"Jimmy," Ellen said. Her hands hovered about him, his distress growing. He was trembling, collapsing into another seizure. *Damn it,* she thought, and she took James' hand.

She was hit with a wall of sensations. Complete darkness. A horrible stench, the sounds of moaning. Suddenly she could see her own hands covered in puss-filled sores, their surface diaphanous thin and jiggling.

She whispered. "I never… I didn't…"

The two of them sat together on the bench, shuddering, their eyes locked together. They did not move for several minutes. Abruptly, they each took deep, lunging breaths, breathing in unison while passing pedestrians, cars and busses obscured their silent struggle with layers of passing humanity.

Ellen woke on one of the two couches in the front room, recalling everything at once. It was well after midnight. With a start, she recalled James was sleeping on the second couch. She had returned to the house and collapsed, the experience on the bench leaving her utterly exhausted.

Many times in her career she had done crisis support work. In her internship at the hospital this had included suicidal clients and victims of traumatic accidents, violence, people in crisis, flailing to gain some purchase on a path forward in the most terrible of circumstances. But what had happened when she took James' hand had left her utterly depleted, an exhaustion of the soul. It began as a wall of felt experiences, visions, intense physical pain that filled her body and then moved through, taking her strength, her vitality with it. The deep exhaustion it left behind was intensified by an overwhelming mix of grief, rage, despair. Her initial instinct was to believe that her emotions were vastly out of scale, but then, she realized they were not. Not for her and not for those who were the source of them.

She kept an eye on James, shocked that he had been in the room with her as she slept. But there he was, on the other couch, which he had dragged across the room to get as far away as possible from her.

She thought through the things she experienced in front of the deli. A place she had walked past thousands of times. It was a street corner she knew intimately, every crack in the sidewalk, every curbstone. She could feel the sores swarming across her hands and arms, across her back, but now when she looked at her hands, they were clear and unblemished.

James moaned and settled again. She checked her watch. It was 4:15. She heard distant sirens, growing louder. Two police cars raced past in front of the house. Blue and red light splashed across the wall, receding as the sirens faded. She closed her eyes, exhaustion returning to wash over her.

She felt a hand on her head.

"Jimmy, *don't,*" she snarled, adrenaline surging up in her. She jerked about onto her back, balling up her fists, prepared to fight. It was not Jimmy. Her father stood over her, slowly shaking his head. His expression sorrowful, lost. Again, he slowly shook his head no. For a few moments, Ellen simply took him in. Her calm therapist self marveled at him, at the change in his demeanor. His stoic and impenetrable lack of connection now shifted to deep sadness. She had only seen it once. For a few moments on the day he had shown up drunk. And now here it was again. She took a breath and whispered.

"Jimmy."

The house remained silent. The figure before her unmoving. She spoke again more loudly. "Jimmy, wake up."

James sat up on one elbow and spoke. "What does he want?"

"I don't know," she answered.

"He wants something from you, it's obvious," James said.

Ellen's father bent down toward her, reaching out his hand to touch her again. She recoiled. The figure straightened and looked at her for a moment longer. Then it turned and disappeared down the dark hallway.

"They all want something," James said.

"He had nine months to ask me for anything." Her voice was ragged with exhaustion.

"Why are you so angry at him?" James asked.

"I don't know. Nothing. Everything," she said after a moment.

"So, he wants you to forgive him?" James asked.

"I don't know," she repeated.

"So maybe just forgive him. Unless you want him to suffer some more, first," James said.

"I don't know why he's here. All right? Honestly, I'd be hard pressed to tell you why he was ever here."

Trapped, she thought to herself. *Its all a trap.* "I'm not answerable to you or him, Jimmy," she said, her voice cold. She didn't name it, but a word hung unspoken.

"Fine. If he comes back, deal with it yourself. I need some sleep," James rolled over, turning his back to her.

Ellen opened her eyes. The sun was streaming in. James was not on the couch. She rose and walked to the hallway. James was sitting on the floor with his back to a closet door.

"Here I was, busy trying to understand how so many of them were stuck in this house. But clearly, it's not this house they're stuck in?"

"Ah," Ellen said. "It's something that was here before."

Chapter 15

Ellen and Jimmy were in the historical documents section of the San Francisco Public Library. It was located somewhere in the labyrinthine basement of the vast old building. They were surrounded by stacks and flat file cabinets that marched in ranks into the distance. Buzzing fluorescent lights hung in long rows overhead. Jimmy had an unlit cigarette in his mouth. Before them on a large table were various books and documents they had pulled from the bookshelves over the course of the morning. One large ledger was open before them.

At the top of the page, it read in long-hand script, *City of San Francisco, Deeded Properties, 1884*. He turned to another page. A large map showed part of downtown San Francisco and surrounding neighborhoods. The map was hand drawn, with lot numbers marked in elegant curving digits. Jimmy ran his finger down streets until he came to a specific spot.

"Hm," he said. "It's not a house lot. It's bigger." He noted the block and lot number and turned back a few pages.

"The Empress Hotel," he said. "It took up several lots. He flipped back to the map page. Its foundations ran south to east."

"Across behind the deli," Ellen said.

Ellen and Jimmy sat before one of the library's computer terminals. On screen, several periodicals and book titles had come up in response to their search on the Empress Hotel.

"Empress Hotel was a popular name. British Columbia. England. La Jolla. Okay, here's an old book on San Francisco, *Hotels of the City: A Survey by Nelson Carlton*. 1879," Jimmy said.

"Anything else?" Ellen asked.

"Doesn't look like it," Jimmy replied.

They walked to the corresponding flat file and Ellen drew open the drawer. There were pamphlets in clear plastic sleeves.

"Here it is," she said. "It's just a booklet."

They took it to a table and slid it out of the sleeve.

"A tourist's guide of some kind. It's alphabetical," she said. "Here." She began reading, "The Empress is a 120-room hotel, built in 1855. The hotel has a lovely stone facade, electric lights and an electric elevator. It is built on the remains of the original Hotel Empress that burned in the great fires that swept the city on May 4th, 1851. The Hotel Empress overlooked Yerba Buena Cove, prior to the cove's being filled. The Empress remains a sturdy and admirable working man's hotel but is not recommended for persons of greater refinement."

She ran her finger along the screen. "The waterfront came right up into the neighborhood before they filled it in. But what does any of this tell us?"

Jimmy scratched his chin. "The previous hotel was destroyed in a fire."

A librarian passed and stopped to frown at the unlit cigarette in Jimmy's hand.

"I'm not gonna light it," he said, irritably.

She walked on.

"Who are you talking to?" Ellen asked.

"I need a smoke," Jimmy said, rising.

Outside the library, Jimmy puffed furiously on the cigarette.

"There was a librarian in the building. She stood there and she looked at me. She saw I was holding a cigarette," he said.

"Just now?" Ellen asked.

"She looked right at me. They don't do that. It doesn't happen."

"Are you doing something different? Not drinking?" Ellen suggested.

"Fuck! I'm not drunk every day, Ellen. I'm telling you they don't do this. I've only seen it once or twice before. Now, I've seen it happen multiple times in the last few days. The doctor in the hospital. Your father, in the house, yesterday."

Ellen lit a cigarette and turned away from him, several reactions coming in quick succession to Jimmy's ever-increasing role as a confirming witness. It was introducing an uncomfortable intimacy between them.

"I don't understand any of it," he said, anger flaring in his voice.

It was like a switch flipping, the way his anger flared up. Then, just as quickly, she saw it drop away, shifting to resignation or perhaps, disinterest. He had a startling capacity to instantly suppress dangerous emotions, like he was dropping them down a well. No doubt born out of rigid self-protection, of not drawing attention from those around him. *How young was he when he learned that trick?* she thought.

In her therapy work, she understood trauma to be a combination of elements. Trauma is an event or events, but it is equally determined by what follows, by the meaning that gets made about the events, meaning made in relationship to those around us. What Jimmy dealt with was impossible to seek support for. To admit, at any time in his life, the source of the trauma, invited exactly the wrong kind of interventions. Interventions that compound the damage.

If she had met him prior to her father's death, there would have been any number of diagnoses she would have applied to him. Like every psychologist he had seen in his life, she would have referred to the Diagnostic and Statistical Manual of Mental Disorders, probably starting with schizophrenia and adding on from there. Filling in insurance forms with codes and billing rates. Submitting his madness as a string of numbers and letters, never doubting the efficacy of locating the problem in him, and only in him.

Now she was in the exact same danger he was, a danger not from the dead but from the living. Of telling anything to the wrong person. One diagnosis written on one insurance form would be enough. Bi-polar, schizophrenic, what did it matter? Any such diagnosis and her hard-earned independence would start slipping away. Her practice would be at risk. Her carefully curated client list, along with the identity she had carefully built. An identity which, truth be told, was already crumbling.

Jimmy had become increasingly agitated. "If I know what happened to them ... something of what happened, maybe I won't be caught off guard by what's there. Now, it's like a goddamned jack-in-the-box with the crank turning," he said.

Ellen studied the side of his face. It was a curious thing, to study a stranger's face this closely. We spend our lives learning something so central. Look at a person for a few moments too long and they will look back, notice us.

But Jimmy cannot look back at us, she thought. Not without pulling the veil off the shadows that swarm around us. Not without triggering that ugly hint of knowing; that we are all in a world of something more, something else, *others.*

He's no different than the rest of us, she thought. Billions of us avoiding eye contact because of the shadows we know will be revealed in the eyes of strangers. Neediness. Grief. Despair. Violence.

Jimmy's expression was shifting from confusion to irritation and back again. He occasionally gave a small shake of his head, as if over and over he was reaching the end of the train of thought, another dead end, and rejecting it.

"What's going on?" she asked him.

He took a deep breath. It was a choice. Such a simple thing, really. To talk to another person about a problem. Something he had not done in decades.

"People who hire me tell me that their Uncle Bob or Grampa Harry or whoever is dead and is hanging around and could I make them go away. I say please give me X amount of dollars and I'll do it. They agree. I go to whatever location, and I wait for Grampa Harry to show up. I approach Grampa Harry. I see a light. They see it. And then they find their way ..."

Jimmy gestured vaguely upward.

"... out."

"They see the light. They don't ever see me. They don't notice me at all. I see the light. They see the light. They go. That's it."

Jimmy flicked his cigarette butt away.

"Sometimes, I get a hint of what's causing them a problem. I get a whiff of some minor regret or another and then they're gone. Occasionally, it can be something worse. Something vile," he said, grimacing. Jimmy gestured for another cigarette from Ellen. She held out the pack for him. She saw that his hand was shaking too much to pick the cigarette out of the end of the pack.

Delirium tremens? she thought. Ellen lit a cigarette and handed it to him, careful to insure he was able to avoid touching her hand.

"At some point, I took to having a couple of drinks, especially when I got a weird vibe from a client. It blunts the impact. Numbs it down," he said. "But this time it didn't help. It left me wide open in my own fucking house."

"What is different?" she asked.

"They can see me." He spit contemptuously on the ground. "Remember when I said your case was the worst I've come across?" He rolled his eyes, exhaling loudly. "When I was a kid, in Texas. There was a whole thing that happened. This feels like that. And it's ramping up like that one did," he said.

He paused and held up his hand as if to ward off a blow, his head dipping and turning away further. "All of this? It started in the bar when you tried to take back your goddamn business card. You touched my hand, and they saw me. And now they haven't stopped looking right at me. I barely got out of the second house."

A bead of sweat ran down along his face.

"For whatever reason, they really hate me. Which makes contact with them bad, like heart attack bad. And if I can't stay in there with them long enough, no light is coming. And if no light comes, they don't go."

He raised his hand to take a puff off the cigarette. It was trembling visibly. He looked at his hand and smiled ruefully.

"I feel them all the time, now," He waved his hand in a vague circle, indicating the space around him. "If we don't figure out what's going on, they're going to get to me. They're already getting to me."

Jimmy laughed out loud. It was a bitter barking laugh. "If you told me two weeks ago I would be afraid to take a drink, I would have said you're crazy. But here we are." He glanced at her. "And the only lead we have is a one-hundred-year-old hotel."

"Well, that's not the only lead," Ellen replied.

Chapter 16

They stood before the door of the house, preparing themselves to enter. Ellen had the key in her hand. The morning had turned to afternoon by the time they had returned. Jimmy looked about him. "I wish I knew what the hell is going on with your porch." Jimmy said. "Can we just have one thing about this house make sense?"

"What do you mean?" she asked.

"There's no activity of any kind out here, right? Why are there all kinds of things going on in the house, and just beyond that gate, and nothing, less than nothing, here?" he said. "What suddenly changed? There was plenty of activity the other night when the white power neighborhood watch showed up. That asshole is probably still having nightmares."

Ellen was noticing James' body language. Just a few moments on the porch and already his shoulders had dropped down, relaxing. His jaw was softening. The edge was coming off his voice.

"Maybe, you should take advantage of it," she said. "Wait here. I'm going to get you a chair."

He was looking at her and she was looking back at him, matter of factly. There was no irising down of sound or light. The sunshine remained the sunshine. For Jimmy, at least for this briefest of moments, it was perfectly normal to be looking at another human being. He noticed that her brown eyes were flecked with gold.

In his years of working for people, none had ever wanted to understand the events they were experiencing. They wanted the problem gone. The minute that happened, they wanted him gone. Ellen's ability to listen to and accept the information he was presenting to her showed startling flexibility. His gaze lingered on the curve of her shoulder. It shocked him. He shook his head and stepped back.

Ellen carefully unlocked the door. She went slowly inside, disappearing from his line of sight. Moments later, she returned to the porch, dragging the big high-backed chair from the front room. She positioned it facing the street and gestured to it. "Take a load off," she said. Jimmy shrugged and sat heavily in the chair.

Then she took out her phone. "I had almost forgotten about this," she said. "I recorded them." She played the recording she had made in the kitchen, days before. The whispering voices faded in and out, the language unfamiliar. When it was finished, she flipped the phone once in her hand and caught it.

"Why didn't you tell me about this?" James said, his tone strangely neutral.

"What's wrong now?" she said.

"I'm just asking why you wouldn't have told me about this sooner." Again his tone seemed very carefully modulated.

Controlling his temper, she thought.

"I forgot I even made it," she replied, preparing for his temper to flare again. The way James kept ricocheting between relative calm and explosive outbursts was wearing her down, reducing her ability to regulate her own emotions. *Jack in the Box indeed, mother fucker*, she thought. After days of being consistently on edge, once again, the few moments of relative calm they had just shared were gone. Her careful therapist side went with it.

"I don't know why you're getting upset. It's a lead," she said.

"It's a lot more than that," James replied.

"Stop being weird, and tell me," she said. His calm affect was unnerving.

"You made a recording of their voices," he replied.

"Yes, I did," she said.

"You did this before we ever met."

"Yes …" she said slowly.

"People see things like this sometimes," he continued.

"Yes, they do," she said.

"Lots of people, actually," he continued.

"I imagine so," she replied.

"So why don't we have thousands of videos of what people see or hear?" he said.

She looked at the phone in her hand.

"You manifested an audible instance of a spiritual event, and you did it before you ever met me," he said.

Ellen abruptly put the phone down on the step next to her, staring at it and then back at Jimmy.

"It's you, Ellen. This isn't just something happening to you. You're happening to it." James said. He paused, proceeding carefully. "May I ask you some questions?" he said.

Something dropped in Ellen's gut. She felt chills running across her arms and back.

"Okay," she said. "All right." Alarm bells began ringing in her head. *Stop this.*

"What came first. Your father? The voices? Or did it all start at the same time?"

Ellen looked down, gathering herself, and then looked back

up. "My father was first."

"How do you feel when he shows up?" James asked.

She chewed her lip.

"I feel angry," she responded.

"Angry how?" he asked.

A long silence passed between them. Ellen found herself caught in a tug of war between what she knew to be self-protection and the vast blind spot that same self-protection had created about her father.

"I hate him," she said.

"When he comes. Does he see you?" James asked.

She chewed the inside of her lip. "Yes. He looks right at me. C'mon Jimmy, he touched me."

"Do you have any sense of what he wants?"

"I don't care what he wants," she said.

James waited for a moment.

"Staying angry at him is not a luxury we can afford," Jimmy replied. "You do understand that, right?"

"Then you make him go," she said, her anger flaring up. "Send him the fuck on. That's what you do, isn't it? I'm paying you. Do your job." she said.

"I tried," he said, then he shifted in the chair, drawing a breath.

"Maybe let's not fight this time," he said.

"Okay, okay," she said, raising a hand. "It's just so hard to resist. There's something about you, Jimmy. Makes me goddamn furious."

"So I've been told," James replied.

James rubbed his face for long moments. Then he continued.

"I met a man five years ago. Like you, he had powerful

abilities. He was another person I should never have come in contact with. Unlike you though, he didn't have Armageddon under his house. His brother had died. This poor bastard had no idea why his brother was still there, staring at him all the time. It's the only other time I've seen the dead looking directly at a client. 'I don't want him here,' he told me. 'I hate him.' And he did. I didn't know what it meant then, but I think I know now. He hated his brother so much that he was holding him from leaving."

"Oh, fuck off Jimmy," she said.

James held up his hand.

She struggled to regain her composure.

"What did you do?" she asked brightly.

"I left. I didn't go back," James replied.

"You just left him there?" she said.

"He's still there."

"Ah. And you can't leave because of my bigger problem." Ellen barked out a laugh.

"You want the truth? I don't see you making the same choice," he replied calmly.

Still controlling his temper? she thought.

"After I met you, I suspected you might have some ability, most people do, but this?" He gestured to the phone. "You and me, we shouldn't have come within a hundred miles of each other."

Again, he paused to collect himself. She watched him, noticing the little human tells about him, his posture, his jaw flexing, his deep breaths.

It's not anger. It's fear. He's controlling his fear, she thought. With that, her anger leaked away.

"I don't know what's going on between you and your father, but next time he shows up? Settle things with him. We have a much bigger problem. And if we don't figure this out, someone is going to get killed and I'm pretty sure it won't be you."

A fly landed on James' cheek. He slapped it violently.

Over the course of the conversation, time had slowed way down for Ellen. Surging emotions showed up as wrenching tightness in her gut and chest, corresponding with thoughts boiling, tumbling past, one after another. Her expression twitched. Now it was she who was following threads of ideas to dead ends and rejecting them. The ones she wasn't rejecting were not easy to hold.

"I assume you have friends at the university?" James finally said. "You should have someone translate that." He pointed to her phone. "Sooner rather than later."

"Then let's go," she said.

"Not me," he replied. "I need a break."

"Good idea," she said. She promptly walked down the steps and out the gate, dialing her phone as she went. In a moment, she was gone.

James sat in the chair watching the movement of cars and people on the street. Behind him a fly landed on the inside of the window. Then two. Then thousands.

James rose from the chair and turned to the window. He placed his hand against it. The flies tumbled over each other to get to where his hand was, swarming into a writhing mass on the other side of the glass.

"Hm," he said under his breath.

A sound behind him made him turn. There on the rail of the porch sat a crow, its head cocked sideways. On seeing it, James flattened himself against the window, the flies on the other side of the glass forming a halo around his head. He stared at the bird, his lips drawing back off his teeth.

"No," he said, shaking his head. He slid down to sit heavily on the porch, all the while holding up his hand, blocking the bird from sight. He closed his eyes, lost in waves of memories he had tried all his life to forget. The crow watched him with its dead empty eyes.

Chapter 17

The university halls were full of students, moving in a constant ebb and flow along the hallways. Ellen entered the office of the world languages department and spoke to young man seated at a desk.

"Hi. I'm Ellen Perry. I have an appointment with Annette Garcia."

He led her down a hallway to a room with several workspaces separated by dividers. A woman rose to meet her.

"Hello, Ellen," she said.

"Thank you for seeing me, Annette. I won't take too much of your time."

"I don't have class for another hour. How can I help you?"

Ellen took out her phone and laid it on the desk. She took a breath and began. "My father was a short-wave radio buff, and he left this recording of one of the signals he picked up. I'm writing up something about his work and I want to try and figure out what language this is."

"Oh," Annette said. "A language mystery."

"May I play it for you?"

"Go ahead," Annette replied.

Ellen hit play and the hiss of the recording began. Faint voices drifted in and out, overlapping, fading and rising.

"It's very faint," Annette said leaning in closer, turning her head.

"It gets louder," Ellen replied.

Annette glanced up at Ellen, looking puzzled.

"They sound upset," she said.

"Yeah," Ellen replied. "That's what made me curious about it."

Annette continued listening, her expression reflecting some discomfort. The recording ended and she sat up.

"I'm a romance language expert, so I'm not the ideal person. If I were to guess I'd say maybe an Arabic root? I can ask Leyla. She might be able to tell us. I can also put it on the list serve.

"Um, I'd rather not, in case it's something that might upset people," Ellen demurred.

"Yeah, okay," Annette replied. "How did you say your dad got this?"

"Shortwave. I don't know how long ago. He had it on a cassette tape." Ellen replied. "Crazy, huh? Here. I'm emailing you the audio file."

"I'll get back to you," Annette said.

Chapter 18

It was late. A single lamp next to Ellen cast light across the floor, leaving James mostly in shadow. The two of them sat in silence, each on the couches at opposite sides of the front room.

Ellen worked on her laptop. The only sound was the tapping of the keys. As she worked, she was mindful of a steep drop in James' energy. Exhaustion or possibly depression seemed to be settling over him again. Finally, she closed the laptop.

"This is getting us nowhere," she said. "I've done searches everywhere I know to search. University research databases, major libraries, historical societies. Whatever there is on the Empress Hotel, we've already found it." She rubbed her eyes. "All we have is an audio recording and the name of a hotel."

James didn't respond.

"Jimmy, what is going on with you?"

"That's not all we have," he finally said.

She turned her attention to him, realizing that she had been actively avoiding engaging. *I'm so sick of his up and down bullshit,* she thought. The simple brutality of the thought shocked her. She cast about for her therapist side, for any kind of curiosity. There was only frustration. She waited.

James gestured toward the back of the house. "They're right there waiting for us," he said. He had to marshal all his courage to simply say the words. His entire life had been a rigid exercise in avoidance. Avoiding people. Avoiding the law. Avoiding the drifting shadows always there, visible just out of the corner of his eye. Shadows always there for a reason; trapped, unable to move on, shackled by some ugly aspect of the human heart, warped by cowardice, grief, violence or perhaps a single shocking turn of bad luck; unable to see the light, to leave. And so, for a lifetime, everywhere in the world James looked was not where he wanted to be looking. His rigid practice of avoidance had left him with a terrible watchful anxiety. It stayed with him, receding, rising but only ever gone for a brief interlude when he got to the bottom of a bottle; trading his damaged body for a few moments of numbness.

But no more even of that, he thought. The ones in this house? They had hunted him into his home and stripped him of his oblivion, following him down into the bottle. Now his defenses would have to be marshalled there as well.

"What else do we have?" She said, a second time, more loudly. James looked up.

"I have to take another look," he replied, pointing toward the kitchen. "I have to go back down." Anxiety rolled up his body in a wave, lashing about within him, seeking somewhere to resolve itself, finding only a mass of blood, meat, and bone. Going against his lifetime of self-protection, challenging his deeply entrenched patterns felt like the loss of self entirely. Fight or flight rising, then the urge to lash out. A primal panic against any kind of change, even as his lifetime of self-protection provided ever-decreasing returns with ever-increasing costs, incrementally shifting from what was once protection to something else entirely.

"Okay. What we've seen so far. Can we go over it?" she asked him. "I'll start," she suggested.

"All right," he said.

Ellen went to a side table and took out a yellow notepad. She found a Sharpie. She returned and sat.

"A few days after my father dies, the first thing happens upstairs. I hear my father's television turn on. It gets really loud. I turn it off, but it keeps happening, so I unplug the TV. It keeps happening anyway. It's always the sports shows he used to watch when he was dying. That came first. Within a few days, I start smelling his shit again. All of that is ongoing. It happened even a few days ago upstairs."

"Next, downstairs in the kitchen, I start hearing voices. It starts maybe ten days later." She is writing on the notepad, adding dates. "A few more days, and then I see my father. The door to the basement stairs opens on its own. He's on the stairs to the basement. The door slams. That also keeps happening. He makes such loud noises. TVs, door slamming. Like he's trying to scare me."

"May not be him," James replied. She glanced up at him. He was sitting forward, eyes closed, his palm pressed against his forehead, his chin down against his chest.

"You want to go out to the porch?" she suggested.

"Keep going," was all he said.

"A few days later, I go to the basement to do laundry. The washer moves. The whispering comes. This happens three different times over several days," she said.

Now James is looking directly at her. He shakes his head. "Jesus, Ellen." he says.

"What?" she says growing increasingly irritated.

"Go on," he said.

"No, I want to know what you mean," she responded.

James returned to pressing his palm against his forehead, his chin to his chest. "First time you've told me that your washing machine was moving," he said.

Ellen paused. She felt her anger drain away. She spoke in a low voice. "If I told you in the bar, you might have saved yourself from all of this," she responded.

"I might have," he replied.

Damn it, she thought, shame coming in.

"I'm sorry, I didn't know what any of it meant. I still don't know. I'm sorry," she said quietly.

"Keep going," he said.

"The last time the washing machine moves I see a girl at the back of the basement. She's in silhouette, so I can't see any details of her. When she came, the washing machine got destroyed."

"Silhouette?" he asked.

"Yeah," she said.

"And when I was down there?" he said, his voice wavering.

"When you collapsed. I saw a different figure. Same place, in the back. They're always completely in silhouette. It was a man. He had … At least it looked like … like he had multiple compound fractures in his arms."

"Silhouette, but a clear distinct outline?" Jimmy asked.

"Yes," she replied.

"And he was there when I was unconscious?"

"Yeah. Also, he was naked, I think. I think they both are," she replied. Gathering herself, she continued. "Then, there was the doctor at the hospital," she said.

"In silhouette?" he asked.

"No. Not at all. He looked normal. I thought he was your doctor. He came and went," she said. "Just like my father, I could see him clearly." She took a breath and continued writing on the pad. "There are the shadows I see when you and I make eye contact," she said. "They are very cloudy. Almost not there. I saw them in the bar, at the take-out place, at the diner that night and I see them here whenever we make eye contact."

"Except on the porch," he said.

"Right, not on the porch."

She paused and sat back, drawing a long breath. "And then there is what I saw when I took your hand on the bench."

James looked up; his blue eyes bright in the dim light. "Describe that."

"It's dark. I'm lying on my back. I'm unable to sit up. Something is holding me down. I hear cries all around me. People in pain. The voices are in a language I don't understand. Then, in the dark, a child's hand takes mine. I hear rasping, bubbling. Like the child is suffocating."

"Drowning …" he said.

"Yes, exactly," she replied. "Then, we were back on the bench. You were there looking at me. There was this terrible pain. I looked down at my hands. There were sores all over my hands and arms. Each one felt like a cigarette burn. As if someone had burned me every few inches all over my arms and back. And I was choking, like there were hands around my neck squeezing. And then, all of it was gone, and my hands were normal."

"You're the conduit," he said.

"What does that mean?" she asked.

"I saw exactly the same things after you touched my hand in the bar," he said. "Aside from some of it in a dream, I didn't see it again until you grabbed my hand on the bench. In the basements, all I see are shadows, fog, nothing distinct. You have the stronger connection. You are seeing them much more clearly. They're connected to you, but they want me dead. I don't know why but their hatred is palpable. If I don't get away, it's overwhelming," he continued.

"Overwhelming how?" she asked.

"I feel, pressure. Immense heat and pressure …" His voice trailed off. "It was coming on again in the second house. So I ran, but it didn't help. When I got to the bench, they were overwhelming me again. I could feel them in my head. And then you took my hand, and I was in the dark. The child's hand, the voices. Exactly like you describe. And something else was going on. The ground was slowly moving. Then we were back on the bench, and I saw you holding my hand. Just like you describe, I felt the sores on my hands, I couldn't breathe, and then it was over."

"But not entirely …" she said.

"No," he said.

"Really not at all. I'm so angry now. It's all I can do to keep it in check," she said, a grim edge entering her voice.

"That's not what I'm feeling," James replied.

"What then?" Ellen asked.

"Terrified," he said, reaching for the cigarettes. He took one from the pack. As he raised it to his lips, it visibly shook. He lit the end and tossed the lighter back onto the low table in front of him. "We're running out of time. Things are getting worse."

James glanced toward the crow perched outside on the rail of the porch, its form barely discernable against the pattern of dark houses across the way.

They lay on the couches. It was now past 3 a.m. Ellen's deep breathing was audible. She was asleep, but James was not. He was thinking of himself speaking. Of himself saying the words, that they needed to go back into the basement. Each time he ran the actual words through his mind, he flinched.

I have to go back down.

Flinch.

I have to go back down.

Flinch again.

And the darkness came down on him. This thing happening now? It was a private thing. Like a lover we should never have taken. Like a victim we should never have attacked. It was a thing never to be shared with others. It closed in on him, a loathsome suffocation he had endured all his life. It came in the quiet terrible moments between what came before and what was coming next. It drifted in on silent feet to overlay the boredom of waiting and worrying.

I have to go back down.

It roiled up alive in his belly and chest, wrestling its way up his throat to his flesh and face, spreading. It felt so utterly familiar, the filed-sharp teeth of a despair come again and again to his child's bed in the private dark.

How unfair it was. How had such shadow come to have this agency in his life? James wondered again, as he often did, if dying would stamp it out. Or would dying just be more ugly howling leading nowhere? Anger flickered somewhere in him, shifting to grief, and then numb disgust, like a pebble skipping across black waters. None of these little sparks of self mattered, the pebble would stop skipping. Sink. Be swallowed up.

Surely life was meant to be something more. Your body screaming for you to flee but the cage is shut, the door barred, no place in the world is far enough. And so he sat in the darkness, in his faltering determination to go back down into the basement, forever alone with what it invoked in him. He felt it moving, reptilian in his gut. *Trapped.* Accepting that, there were no longer any passing thoughts of dying. No thoughts of drinking himself into oblivion again and again. Nothing could limit the immensity of it. It was a fool's parlor trick, dying, because just beyond dying, it still waited.

Ellen's phone rang. The sun was well up. She rose on one elbow.

"Hello Annette," Ellen said. "Thanks for getting back to me. Any news?" She listened for a few moments. "Okay, well, that would be great. I really appreciate it." There was another pause. "Oh, yeah? Well that's odd. Okay. I really appreciate all your effort. Yeah, it does get your curiosity up, right? Yeah. Well, let me know." She hung up the phone.

James sat across from her.

"You don't look so good," she said.

"Hm," he replied.

"Annette at the university is looking into the recording. She thought it might be an Arabic language, maybe, but now they're not so sure. But they're reaching out to another professor. She did say one thing, though."

"What's that?" James replied.

"They think it's more than one language," she replied.

Chapter 19

James and Ellen stood in the front hallway. Sunlight streamed in through the windows of the house. Up the length of one window, a trailing vine of morning glories created a string of pink and purple blossoms trembling silently in the exterior breeze.

Ellen was in front of James. She looked back over her shoulder at him. His expression was blank.

"You sure you really want to do this?" she asked.

"You can't keep asking me that," he replied.

"Tell me what's going on for you. Every step of the way," she replied, turning to face forward. "If it feels likes it's getting out of control and we turn around, immediately" she said, taking a step into the hallway. "This is our first try. Let's just to get a sense of how far you can go before trouble starts, okay?"

"Just go," he said. And then he also took a step.

Ellen was thinking of the relative ease with which she moved through the house, even recently. Were those below somehow used to her presence? Was James a stranger to them? She passed the mirror in the hall. Glancing to see the mass of dark curls framing her face.

"Nothing so far," James said from behind her.

They crossed the threshold into the kitchen.

"Okay, wait," James said.

"What is it?" she said quietly.

"Not sure," he replied. "Let me stay here for a minute."

Ellen noticed her breath rising and falling and took a deeper breath, attempting to calm herself. Out the back windows, the yard was overgrown, a tangle of tall grasses and rose bushes. Her father's first wife had planted them. It was an odd moment, realizing how little she knew of that woman. The woman was dead and there were these rose bushes. That was it.

"Okay," James said.

"Not enough information," she replied not looking back.

"Um, just a sense of something pulling," he replied. "Down. Same as before."

She turned and saw sweat beading up on his brow. His eyes were aglow, shocking blue.

"Should we leave?" she asked.

"I don't know," he said.

"If you don't know, I sure as fuck don't know," she whispered.

"Go across to the couch," he said.

"Okay," she replied.

They walked slowly; their footfalls audible in the silence. They reached the couch, turned slowly, and sat at either end.

"Your kitchen is a mess," he said.

Ellen looked at him. He was turning his head at an odd angle as if listening. He was trembling. Now his eye was twitching.

"It's a pull, but not ..." His hand began to convulse.

"Nope," she said, and she took his hand.

Marty rang the doorbell again. "She knows we're coming," he replied. He stood on the porch with Anne, another therapist from Ellen's office. They had worked with Ellen for years in the comfortable cadences of the practice.

Marty was in his fifties. With his disheveled paunch, he was used to putting others at ease, invoking a harmless demeanor that hid a powerful, analytical mind. Anne was in her late sixties, her hair short-cropped, her large, colorful necklace and bright jacket a study in professional style. She was a deeply compassionate woman whose practice included pro bono work for clients at the San Francisco women's shelter. Marty shifted his feet and reached for the doorbell as the front door swung open.

"Marty," Ellen said, her voice bright, if a bit loud. "Would you excuse me?" she said. She stepped between the two of them out onto the porch with James in tow. Marty and Anne turned as they passed through, Ellen holding James' hand. The two turned to face the new arrivals, Ellen continuing to hold James' hand with firm determination.

Marty studied the man with Ellen. He wore a rumpled and disheveled plaid shirt that looked as if he had been sleeping in it. His face had the blotchy look of a heavy drinker. But both Marty and Anne were focused on what the man was doing. He was taking deep gulps of air, as if he had been running or holding his breath.

"You all right?" Ellen said to him.

"Yeah," he said. Then, as if they were only now noticing, they slowly released their hands.

"Well, here we are," Ellen said to Marty and Anne. She had a slightly wild-eyed look, which was quickly receding. She turned again to James.

"Marty, Anne, this is James," she said.

James held out his hand. Marty shook his hand.

"How are you, James?" Marty said.

"Not bad, all things considered," James replied, glancing at his open hand. "Call me Jimmy."

"I thought you guys were coming by today," Ellen said. "Shall we get some breakfast?" She herded them down off the porch.

"Wait," she said turning back. "I'll just get my bag." She darted back up the stairs and into the house.

James stood looking at them.

"So, James," Anne said. "How do you know Ellen?"

"She hired me to help with the house," he replied.

"Oh, she's doing some repairs?" Marty asked.

"Not that kind of help," James replied.

James had not bothered to look up for several minutes. He was continuing to shovel food into his mouth. He paused once to ask for the butter. Then he put most of it on a roll and went back to eating, effectively masking the fact that he was not making eye contact.

Marty and Anne watched with growing confusion as Ellen quietly ate her breakfast, seemingly immune to the presence of the man next to her. It was as if there were only the three of them at the table.

Anne finally took the bull by the horns.

"Ellen, we're concerned," she said.

James glanced up.

"Well, not concerned, that's not the right word. We'd like to know how you're doing," Anne continued. "I'm so sorry for your loss and I know it was a long time that you were caring for your father, but now I want to know how you're doing. I miss seeing you. I used to see you every day. Now it's been months."

"Yes, that really is the truth of it," Marty said. For a moment his congenial mask slipped. "It's not the same without you, Ellie."

He continued. "We're wondering when you might come back to the office. Covering your clients has gone fine, but at some point, we really want you back. Maybe you could just start with a day or two a week."

Ellen sat back for a moment. Then she reached over and took Marty's hand. "I miss being with all of you, too. I really do. You know I love you two. I do," she said. "I'm … just not ready to come back to work."

"May I ask why?" Anne said.

Ellen sat with the question for a moment.

"It's not easy to say this, but I'm questioning my work," she said. "I'm questioning my motives, my theories, my purpose … all of it. Until I sort that out, I can't see clients. If I did, I wouldn't feel like I have any ethics at all."

There was a pause as Anne and Marty took that in. Then Marty spoke.

"With all due respect, Jimmy," he said.

"Please," James replied, looking past Marty's shoulder.

"Terry told us about a man being at the hospital with you. About you lying to the doctor. Saying he was your cousin. I'm guessing that was Jimmy?" he said.

"Yes, it was," Ellen replied.

"Are you safe with him in your house?" Marty asked, his eyes darting to James and back to Ellen, studying each person's reaction in the flickering first instances after his question. James looked up and away for a second, irritation showing on his face. Ellen never broke eye contact.

"I'm fine. Jimmy is not my issue," she said.

Anne had also been watching them closely. After a moment, she sighed and turned to Marty. "She's going to do what she's going to do," she said, matter-of-factly.

"Then I guess we can finish our breakfasts," Marty replied.

Marty and Anne got in a cab. As it pulled away, Ellen turned to James. "He's one of my dearest friends, Jimmy. You could have hurt him very badly," she said. "What possible reason could you have to shake his hand?"

"I was on the porch," Jimmy replied. "We needed to know. And … I wanted to see what it was like."

"To what?"

"To shake someone's hand," James replied.

"Damn it," she said. She dropped her head down, her hair falling into her face. She turned her head sideways and set one hand on her hip. "Tch," was the sound she made with her tongue, shaking her head. When she looked up, her face was flushed with emotion.

"I'm sorry you've had to go through what you've gone through. I'm only starting to understand, so please be patient with me."

James looked away. "Hm," he said. "I think I like you better pissed off."

"I can do that," she laughed bitterly. "That I can do."

"So, can we go?" James said, turning sideways to avoid being brushed against by those passing on the sidewalk.

"Yeah, c'mon," Ellen said and they disappeared into the lunchtime crowds.

Chapter 20

Ellen took bread and a few other items to the front of the store. It had been a few days since she was last there. The young Asian man was behind the register. His grandmother was not there.

Ellen waited to one side for James who was still in the back of the store. As she waited, a man stepped up to the register and spoke.

"Where's your grandmother? Not working anymore?" the man said. "That's a shame. She added such an air of slant-eyed appeal to the place."

Ellen turned to see the man from before, standing at the register. As she noticed him, he saw her. He had no items to purchase. He turned casually to her but continued speaking to the young man behind the register.

"Your race traitor friend is here, I see. She should take a lesson from your grandmother." He lurched toward Ellen. "Boo!" he said, laughing. "Grandma knows when to go hide," he said laughing louder.

Ellen stepped back, her arms involuntarily crossing.

"Not so brave today, are you?" the man said, looming over her. "We know who you are, and we know where you live." He slowly raised his hand toward her cheek.

"Don't," she said, setting her jaw. She discretely set her weight on her back leg; glancing left towards the young man behind the counter. He was dialing his phone.

"Now see here's the thing," the man said. "Fear is actually a good thing for women like you to learn."

"Turn around," James said from behind him. "I want you to see this coming."

The man slowly turned to face James.

"Ah, the new boyfriend," he said.

James locked eyes with him. The man made a tiny choking sound, stepping back.

James smiled broadly. "Let's talk about fear, yeah?" He gently put his hand on the man's forearm. There was a moment of contraction. The big man became somehow smaller, as if some part of who he was had suddenly evaporated.

"Mother fucker!" Ellen shrieked. She kicked the man in the back of his knee. A half human cry came from him as he fell back against the checkout counter, both legs giving way beneath him. He threw his arm up to block eye contact with James and then, rolling frantically onto his hands and knees, scrambled on all fours towards the door, rising at the last second to push through and flee.

The man behind the checkout stood staring at the two of them, his cell phone dangling from his hand.

"Damn," he said.

"So stupid to take risks like that," Ellen said, walking up the porch steps. She eyed the street. The young man paused across the way talking on his phone had taken on a very different aspect now. "They know where I live," she said. "For god's sake, he recognized you."

"Hm," James replied.

"It's not safe here anymore," she said, still scanning the

street.

James turned to her. "It's never been all that safe here," he circled his finger in the air, indicating the world around them. "You've just been lucky."

"Don't say that shit to me, Jimmy. You don't know," she replied. She sat on the edge of the porch. He stood at the base of the stairs.

"You have a cigarette?" he asked.

"Have you thought of getting your own pack?" she said.

"I don't smoke that much," he replied holding out his hand. She held out the pack to him. He came up a few steps, took the cigarette and went back down, striking a match as he returned to the walk. She watched him for a moment.

"Why are you suddenly avoiding the porch?" she asked him.

"Have I been?" he said.

"Please," she replied.

"Okay. I just don't like it all that much," he said.

"Why?" she asked.

"It may seem restful to you, but it doesn't to me," he said.

"And why is that?" she asked.

He shrugged. "I don't know. I just don't like it all that much," he replied, turned to look out towards the street.

"You don't like it? Hauling you out here from the kitchen saved you a few hours ago."

"No, that's not what did it," he said. "That anger and hate I keep telling you about? The thing that cooks my head? When you took my hand on the couch, it vanished. Like a light switch. It was totally gone. The porch was a good idea, don't get me wrong, it stops everything, but you made the pressure in my head stop. That was you."

They smoked in silence for a while.

"Why are you hiding things from me?" she asked.

"Because I don't entirely know what's happening.," he said, flatly.

There was another silence.

"Remember when I told you things were getting worse? Today, when you took my hand? You made it possible for me to get closer to them. It's the first piece of good news since I laid eyes on you. The first tiny thing that makes me think I might survive this. But that doesn't mean things aren't getting worse."

"In what way?" she asked.

James paused, thinking hard about what to say next. "That time when I was a kid in Texas," he said. "I told you this was ramping up like that one did?"

"Yeah," she said.

"Well, I have very little understanding of this, mind you. But sometimes when things are big, like this is big? It attracts attention," he said.

"What kind of attention?" she asked.

"Attention we don't want," he said.

She watched him for a moment, suddenly fuming.

"You need to tell me what's going on soon," she said.

He turned away, puffing furiously. Several sparrows swept past in the sunshine. A pigeon made its way along the sidewalk beyond the gate. James made a thorough examination of the yard. Finally, he shrugged and made his way up to the top step and sat at the opposite end from her.

"Thank you for your help in the store," she said.

"Hm," he replied.

They smoked for a bit longer.

"So, we go back down," she said.

"Yeah," he replied. "Holding hands like two kids in kindergarten."

"In that case, can I just say, it's maybe time for you to clean up again?" she said.

"Yeah, sure, fine," he said. "Sorry. Force of habit, looking rough."

"Why?" she asked.

"What's the one thing most people avoid doing with homeless people?" he asked.

"Ah," she said.

She got up and turned toward the door. "I'll leave some clothes for you by the bathroom. And please stop throwing cigarette butts in my yard."

"Is there a razor?" he asked over his shoulder as she walked into the house, the great old door swinging shut.

James looked across the porch, his head dropping low. "Who the fuck is loitering around out here, eh?" he asked to the empty air.

It was after two a.m. James awoke to a muffled shout from Ellen. He opened his eyes to see a man yank her off the couch by her hair, her head hitting the floor with an ugly thump. Then he heard the hammer being cocked on a gun. A figure was standing a foot or so away from the couch, a pistol pointed at his head. Others were in the room, visible in the light of the single lamp.

"Kill that fucking light," a voice said.

James sat up, looking again for Ellen. She was there, near the entrance to the hallway, a man holding her, his hand over her mouth. One of the men yanked the lamp plug out of the wall. The room went dark, lit only by dim light from the streetlight out front.

"Don't let him near you," one of the men said.

"Get the fuck up," the man with the gun said.

James rose from the couch and saw stars flash as he fell hard to the floor. A second man stood nearby with an aluminum baseball bat. James heard Ellen thrashing.

"Don't!" she shouted. The man with the gun stepped over to her and brought the butt of it across the side of her head.

"Shut up or he dies right here," the man with the gun said. "Now get up," he said, turning back to James.

James stood again. He felt something warm running down his neck. The two men were circling to drive him toward the hallway. He felt the hard tip of the bat jam at this lower back.

"Down the hall," the man with the gun said.

James stepped forward, his eyes fixed on Ellen in the dim light. Her eyes were no longer fully open. The man dragged her into the hallway, her legs trailing. Then her legs began moving and she started walking, coming back to consciousness.

There was no talking from these men. No white power bullshit or insults. They wanted them out of the front room as quickly as possible. James glanced back to catch a last glimpse of the empty street beyond the dark windows as he passed through the doorway into the hall. Walking past the dining room, he glanced across to see the glass gone from the center window, the beading apparently cut away and the glass removed from the bottom frame.

They reached the end of the hall, and he was pushed into the kitchen. The basement door was flung wide open. The man who held Ellen was already dragging her through. The tip of the bat hit him hard in the back of the head.

"Move!" the man with the bat said, forcing him towards the

basement door. The pain in his head was excruciating. He had been hit twice, but something else was rising too. He stumbled against the door frame and stepped onto the stairs. The light at the bottom was on.

Below, he saw Ellen being dragged beyond his line of sight. He quickly descended the stairs, ducking his head to keep line of sight on the lower half of her being dragged to the left. He found himself at the bottom, pressure increasing horribly in his head. The man dragging Ellen shoved her towards the front of the basement and stepped back towards the stairs. James felt the bat jam into his back. He stumbled to where Ellen was and turned to face them.

The four men stood across from them. The basement light behind them cast their faces into shadow. James glanced at Ellen. She was looking at the men. She was smiling, a wicked smile punctuated by the red blood streaming down from her temple. *Why is she smiling?* he thought.

One of the men glanced back over his shoulder seeing nothing but an empty basement. But some instinct had warned him. Some small awareness had caused him to look back. One of the other men put his hand to the side of his head absent mindedly, as if there was some discomfort.

Moments passed as the four men gathered themselves for what they meant to do next. The light behind them made it hard to see their expressions, but something was relayed in their postures, in the way their heads turned slightly away. *Why?* they seemed to be thinking. *Why is she smiling like that?*

Then Ellen's hand reached out and took James' and he knew. The moment her hand contacted his, the pressure in his head was gone. He felt her hand as it held his, rising and lowering with the rhythm of her deep breathing. She was leaning slightly forward, anticipating. It was not fear. It was the breathing of a feral animal.

He turned away from her to look back at the men. Beyond them, standing silent, rank on rank, the basement was crowded with figures, diamond-sharp figures cut out of night shadow, silhouettes forming a small army, extending for hundreds of feet beyond where he knew the back wall of the basement to be.

He looked back at Ellen, shocked at the magnitude of what she had created. Of what they had created. The man with the gun raised his pistol. Then, abruptly, his arms fell to his sides. He turned towards the back of the basement, made it a few steps, and collapsed. The other three dropped to their knees, still facing Ellen and James.

"Oh my god," one of them said quietly. Then the four men started screaming. The basement echoed with a deep rhythmic booming. It was what James and heard before, but this time it was not directed at him because she held his hand. Let go of her hand and he would suffer the same fate.

The figures swarmed forward around the men, partially obscuring them. They were buffeted and jerked about. Blood began spilling, red tears running down from their eyes. The side of one man's face was suddenly slashed open, more blood spilling down.

"Ellen!" James yelled over the tumult.

Her tried to turn her his way by her hand as he called her name again, "Ellen!" She did not look at him. Her eyes were wide, her bloody leering grin, ghastly.

"We have to get them out of here," James yelled.

She wasn't hearing or seeing him.

"You want dead bodies down here?" he yelled over the screaming. "What about cops? You want cops here?"

She continued to stare at the screaming men. Finally he yelled, "You can never come back from this!" The men's screams rose in pitch, like some terrible synchronized chorus. Ellen watched for a moment longer, then finally glanced towards James.

"Dammit," she yelled, yanking him forward.

She grabbed one of the men by his upper arm, dragging him to his feet. He clung to her outstretched hand, his eyes rolling up into his head. James, continuing to hold her other hand, pulled a second man to his feet.

The figures were allowing Ellen and any man whose hand she held to pass. Ellen and James stumbled past the man with the gun who lay screaming on the floor and pushed the two men up the stairs. After a few steps, the two men broke and ran upward to the first floor.

Ellen and James turned back. The man with the gun had struggled to his knees and raised the gun to his head, his eyes wide, still screaming.

"No!" James yelled. He lurched forward, yanking Ellen along, and wrenched the gun away from the man's temple, tossing it behind him.

Ellen and James dragged the final two to the stairs. The men staggered up the first few steps and then bolted the rest of the way up and out. And with that, the booming abruptly ended. In the ensuing silence, they heard the men's boots racing down the length of the house and down off the porch beyond.

James started climbing the stairs with Ellen's hand in his. He paused, not looking down behind him. Finally, he steeled himself and glanced back. The space, lit by the single basement bulb, was filled with the silhouettes of figures, male and female, standing in eerie stillness, looking up at him. They were back a small distance, leaving an open space before the stairs.

Alone in that space stood a young child. She raised her hand to him. The simple gesture shocked him to his core. *The child's hand in the darkness.* He quickly dragged Ellen up the stairs and out to the first floor. She was in a trance. Only by his prompting did she make her way up and out. Otherwise, she might have remained among them.

Chapter 21

Ellen was sobbing. It was an ugly raw sound.

James sat across from her on the couch and waited. What else was there to do?

He had set her gently down on the couch. He had closed the front door which had been left wide open, where the men had fled the house. He had stepped around his own blood on the floor of the front room, and hers.

Her head was down, her hair obscuring her face. She had used it that way when she was young. "Tie your hair back, honey, show momma your pretty face," A skinny girl with a mass of hair always in her face. Always obscuring her quick darting eyes.

Something was colliding with a lifetime of meaning-making and carefully constructed rationalizations, brought to light by the rarest of opportunities. The opportunity to extract vengeance.

For most who have suffered abuse, neglect, cruelty, abandonment, that perfect moment of revenge becomes a dearly held fantasy, replayed over and over. A life raft in a sea of shame and self-loathing, a story already aging into irrelevance from the moment it is born. A child's story, to drag into the present that which is already dead and gone in the waning hope that a story forever retold can still be acted on. A final act in a dead and empty theater. A ghost light.

Ellen had seen the trap so many times in the therapy room.

People who could not let go of such stories. And so, she had packed hers away. Sealed them off through hundreds of hours of her own therapy. Through a carefully crafted self-deception of closure, she had packed away the narratives of her early life. A mother who drank and flailed, who had brought her into proximity to men who were savage and dangerous, made her a witness to an unspeakable act of violence, the moment of release, the grief of loss. Handed off with little fanfare to her father's house of stoicism and silence; receiving the cold protection of his gift of nothing shared with no one.

Something vast was breaking through the self-protection that had become Ellen's armor against such memories. After years of constructing, layer on interlocking layer the story that she was in control, the men below had woken a rage so profound that now she was unable to imagine herself having lived with it hidden for so very long. Rage hidden deep within her. Obscured.

Trapped.

In an instant, the barricades of her careful self-control had been overwhelmed. Those men, stand-ins for something else, longer, more deeply rooted, woven into her life by silences that spanned decades, lifetimes.

To have gone from her mother's home to her father's was a special kind of cruelty. But who to blame? Who would pay for the blind and unfathomable cruelty of adults to children, of fathers to daughters, of one human being to another? From a home of endless, unfiltered, angry chatter, to a home of stoic silence, neither one a place in which was she ever heard. Not a word of her voice. Not two moments of understanding or connection to tie together, to build the frailest raft of meaning making for a child. Just broken, towering adults staggering around in their wounded lives. And so, she was left on her own, to build a fortress of protection for herself, and to smother the immense rage of the isolation it required of her.

She had built it to insure she would be safe, yes, but something else was finally arriving. She had built it also to avoid doing harm. To pass no more of her family's trauma on. Not in her own name. Not in the name of her father. Not in the name of her mother. Better to stay separate. And yet, it had failed. She would have let those men die horribly, taken a raw and ugly pleasure from it.

A monster was what she was.

It was then that she felt a hand on her head. She looked up. Her father was standing over her in the dimness, shaking his head, "no," the first light of dawn emerging somewhere in the East, a faint glow in the room.

"Daddy," she said, her self-imposed isolation, her rigid fear of doing more harm, exactly mirroring a lifetime of his.

He looked down at her, still slowly shaking his head no.

And she let him go. And he was gone.

She looked over to James, who all the while had been watching, his eyes glowing a shocking blue. She realized there had been no dawn yet. The light had been his. He rose and got a blanket for her. She lay down and slept deeply.

Chapter 22

The sun poured in through the windows hurting her eyes. Ellen sat upright, nursing the side of her head. There was the possibility of concussion for both her and James, but each, for their own reasons, had decided not to go to the hospital. For a time, they sat silently, simply overwhelmed.

"We went back down," Ellen finally said, not smiling.

"Yes, we did," James said, the memory of the first violent blow to his head lurching up.

"I would have let them die down there," Ellen said.

"But we didn't, and now we don't have corpses to deal with this morning," James replied.

"Right. No corpses before breakfast," Ellen said. "My god, how did it all get so out of control?"

James felt the world closing down. Something was crowding in on him, a half-remembered knowing.

Ellen's phone rang.

"Hi Annette," Ellen said. "Yes, okay. That sounds interesting." Ellen's voice was weak. "I don't know if I can come today."

James chewed his lip.

"I was in a car accident yesterday," Ellen said. The pitch of Annette's voice on the other end of the call rose.

"No, I'm okay, just banged my head," Ellen said.

James waved his hand. "We need information," he said, speaking low. Ellen nodded, grimacing.

"You know, on second thought, it would probably be good for me to get out. Let her know I'll come meet her. Two o'clock, you said? Yeah. Okay. Thanks so much, Annette." She hung up the phone and lay back.

"My head is killing me," she said. After a moment, she rose and went up the stairs. James remained on the couch, marshalling his waning courage. Something very different was happening since they had come up from the basement hours ago. The sense of it triggered vague memories from his childhood. An old and unwelcome understanding was forcing its way to the surface, against all his efforts to resist it, slowly filling his awareness.

He began to go back and pick through his fragmented memories of a night long ago when something terrible had come for him and his young friends in the dark woods of Texas. He had never been fully able to recall the details of what had taken place there. It remained a vague disconnected kaleidoscope, a collection of repressed fragments, like trying to recall a fading nightmare that hides something dark and damaging just out of sight.

Only the events that came after, the shattering of who he was that resulted, were clear to him. The memory of the electroshock table flickered. The wooden dowel between his teeth, the smell of something burning.

I need information, James thought.

And across from him it appeared, standing on the mantle. A great black crow, now inside the house with him, all his hopes for safety evaporating in an instant. The half-remembered thing. It was here.

The crow cocked its head sideways. Ellen was coming down

the stairs. She entered the room, moving slowly, mostly by force of will. "I found these butterfly bandages upstairs," she said. She had washed her face, changed her clothes, and applied a bandage to her temple. The bruise expanded out past it. She set the rest of the bandages on the table and paused.

"Are you okay?" she asked James.

James glanced at the crow. Its black eyes reflected no light, inky wells of nothingness. *A carrion eater*, he thought. "Yeah," he said. Ellen was not seeing what he was seeing, and he did not want her to.

"Okay. Hopefully, we'll get some information we can use," she said. "I'll bring back something to eat." She shouldered her bag and walked out of the house, closing the big front door behind her.

"You asked," a voice said from somewhere in the house. A voice made of tree bark and cold rain.

Then something very old took hold in James. The part of him that lived without hope, without any expectation of help. Formed in the asylum, fired in the darkness of the bottle, in the emptiness of absolute isolation. The part of him that had emerged in the past days, a product of his time with Ellen, retreated. Some deep-seated part, came forward. The nihilist. The dead man.

The fear that had been clutching at his heart fell away. It beat strongly now, the stroking of a clock at midnight. He reached for the pack of cigarettes on the table. The crow spread its wings, becoming a vast shadow across the side of the room.

"And what's this going to cost me?" he said, lighting one.

Annette knocked on the door of the office and then opened it. Behind her, Ellen waited, a butterfly bandage on her temple, purple bruising visible.

"Karla?" Annette said as she and Ellen entered.

An older woman rose from her desk to greet them. "Annette, it's lovely to see you, and you must be Ellen," Karla said. Her marked accent was Norwegian.

"That is quite a bruise," she said to Ellen.

"Someone ran a red light, caught my car crossing the intersection. I banged into the door frame. It looks worse than it is."

"Well, come in and sit down," Karla said. Annette and Ellen sat in the two chairs in front of the desk. "Can I get you anything?" Karla asked.

"I'm fine," Ellen said. Annette shook her head no.

Formalities completed, Ellen began.

"Thank you for looking into our little language mystery. I'm very grateful," she said.

"Annette and I do love a mystery. And your recording certainly is that. That said, to my knowledge, it's not a known language." she said. "Annette said your father recorded it off a shortwave radio?"

"That's right," Ellen said. *When did I start lying so much,* she thought.

"Do you know how long ago?" Karin asked.

"I'm sorry, honestly, I'm just guessing maybe in the 1970s. He had it on a cassette among his things."

"I ask because it's either a very complex prank or it's a previously unknown language. If it's a prank, it's a pretty sophisticated one. For example, the tempo and the patterns suggest an underlying language structure. Never mind the wide range of different voices and the emotional charge. It's more like a dramatic production of some kind than a prank. But it's equally strange if its authentic," Karin replied.

"So it might be a prank," Ellen replied. "But if it's not?"

"If it's authentic, what these people are speaking is some form of language isolate," she said. "One that no longer exists."

"What's a language isolate?" Ellen asked.

"It refers to a language that has no demonstrable genetic relationship to any other language. Examples would include Basque in Europe; in Asia there is Ainu; in Africa, Sandawe. Here in North America we have Haida and Zuni. There is Kanoê in South America, Tiwi in Australia. How many there have been, we'll never know," Karin said. "Such languages are possibly the last remaining branch of a language family that was once more common."

"An entire language could have disappeared that recently?" Ellen asked.

"Sadly, yes. Dozens of languages may disappear in India alone, over the course of the next generation or two."

"Is there any way to locate this one geographically?" Ellen asked.

"Well, not the isolate. But that's not the only language being spoken here. There is a little bit of a language we do know."

"And it's Arabic?"

"No," Karin said. "It's an Afroasiatic language; specifically, Hausa."

Ellen felt a chill settling on her. "And where is that spoken?" she asked.

"Northern Nigeria, Southern Niger, Southern Chad, the Central African Republic, Cameroon," Karin replied.

"What are they saying?"

Well, it's faint, and there's only a brief phrase, but as far as I can tell, they're repeatedly calling out *shaidannu*," Karin said. "It's the Hausa word for devils."

Chapter 23

By the time Ellen returned home, the sun had dropped behind the houses across the way, casting shadows on the porch of the house. She opened the door and went inside. James was not there. She was alone. She stood listening. Then, she squared her shoulders, dropped her bag, and walked down the long hallway to the kitchen. The light in the house was waning, shifting to deeper blues and purples.

The kitchen was as she had left it. She drew a deep breath, slipping back into the long days she had spent alone before James first entered the house. A strange nostalgia rose in her for those days of absolute isolation. She went to the couch and turning to examine the basement door, sat. She lit a cigarette.

"C'mon, then," she said.

James sat in a bus shelter. Light flooded out of the windows of a grocery store behind him. A misty rain was falling. The streets were empty. The great wings of the crow swept past down the center of the street, banking to show its wingspan, darkness on raining darkness.

"C'mon then," he said.

There was a light flickering of the air, and the colors around James shifted. Behind him, the grocery store was now a towering Victorian house, its windows glowing faintly. James rose and turned to face it. *Candlelight?* James thought. *Why bother?* He found himself feeling irritable.

He walked up the steps of the house to the great double doors, raised the heavy brass knocker and dropped it. A deep boom echoed through the house. After a moment, the door opened, and a wizened old man stood blocking the way. He was bent almost double. He wore an old suit coat, cut in a style long gone. His nose was bulbous and hooked downward, or was it? To look directly at him was to invite confusion, his features not so much shifting as unmemorable in each passing moment that one looked.

"I need information," James said.

"You flush?" the old man asked.

"What you see here," James replied.

"Always happy to help a fellow traveler," the old man said.

"The fuck you are," James said.

"I'd advise you to keep a civil tongue in your head," the old man said.

"Grant me my little delusions of freedom, yeah?" James said. The old man opened the door of the vast old house for James to enter.

They passed several rooms, their great doors closed and locked, and entered a library, its shelves stacked with leather-bound books floor to ceiling. The shelves disappeared upward into the dimness beyond the light, so overloaded they gave the impression they were all about to collapse on whomever was in the room. The old man took up his place behind a great, dark desk piled with books and manuscripts. The crow settled on the top of the high-backed chair that dwarfed the old man.

"Not that I'm not happy to see you, but I'm busy here," the old man said. He pushed a few things aside on the great desk and

126

folding his fingers neatly together, placed his hands on the cleared space before him. "Ask," he said.

"First we talk about payment," James said.

The old man's tongue flicked about his lips. "There's a lot happening in that house. Invite me into the basement and your fee is paid," the old man said.

"No," James said.

"You don't say that to me, wretched thing," the old man said. The desk and the high-backed chair were now empty. "They'll be the end of you," a deeper voice said from somewhere in the shadows above. "The fee gets paid either way."

"I pay you now," James said.

The air flickered and the old man was back, his tongue moving slowly across his lips. "You?" he said.

"What will you take from me in order to give me what I need?" James said.

The old man squirmed in his chair.

"A week of your life," the old man said, his voice crackling with unfiltered gluttony. The crow casually spread its wings above, casting long shadows across the books.

James paused and studied the old man. "An hour," he replied.

"Preposterous! Three days," the old man replied, indignant.

"An hour," James replied. "It's all you'll get, so take it."

The old man studied him, drawing back slightly. Saliva escaped from one side of his mouth, running down his chin.

"What makes you think you can bargain with me?" the old man said.

"I've met your kind before," James said. "And I struck a poor deal. I won't be making that mistake today."

"I could splay your guts out and dance in them," the old man said, shivering with pleasure.

"Maybe once. But no one comes here anymore, do they?" James said, musing. "What a small thing you've been reduced to."

"You tempt me?" the old man said.

James looked around. "Awfully quiet here," James said. "Are you so ready to go back to that?"

"Ask your question!" the old man barked.

"You'll take payment first," James said.

"That's not necessary," the old man said in a honeyed tone.

"I won't have a debt to you. I won't have you coming in my last hour. It's enough that you feed on suffering like a leech, you'll take payment now," James said rising from his chair.

"Payment then," the old man said, his tongue darting like a snake's.

"One hour," James repeated.

"One hour," the old man said.

A gold coin appeared on the desk before James. He picked it up, turning it over in his hand. The surface was grimy and scratched. A payment more often rudely taken than willingly given. He placed it on the table and pushed it toward the old man.

The old man's hand darted out with uncanny speed and the coin was gone. A second later, the hand darted out, returning the coin.

"It has no value," the old man bleated.

"Too late," James said, "You took payment."

The old man's chair was again empty. A voice rolled down like thunder from the shadows above. "You'll not cheat me!" the voice said. The bookshelves began to shake. Something crashed to the floor on the other side of the room. The crow set up a racket from his perch on the chair.

"Why bother with all this?" James said. "Answer my question."

The room was silent.

"Tell me about the first Hotel Empress," James said.

The old man was back at his desk.

"Did you know when you struck the deal that you're not alive when you come here?" he said, ducking his head, peevish.

"I do now," James replied.

"Ah, well then, you have cheated me twice. As for the Empress," the old man replied. "Lots of stories about that place in its heyday."

"Places," James replied.

"Yes, well, the early days. The gold rush was a fever on every man, racing to get off the ships, to get to the gold fields. Cheap wooden buildings thrown up on every street corner as fast as they could get their hands on lumber to build them. Red murder everywhere. It's no surprise the city burned down half a dozen times, the Empress along with it, but never entirely. They just kept repairing it, enlarging it. So, technically same hotel."

"What was there at the beginning?" James said.

"You may not like that very much. Not a nice place, that," the old man said, cocking his head sideways, birdlike.

"I won't argue with you there, but I'm not in a position to choose," James replied, sweat running down his face.

"Ah, I see now," the old man said. "Not so nice is it, paying other's debts."

"The first Hotel Empress," James repeated growing dizzy.

The old man was gone. His voice drifted down from above. "Come see me again and we'll discuss it further…"

James sat, bent forward on the bus stop bench. "Dammit," he

said pushing himself upright. His face was soaked with sweat. He was utterly exhausted, struggling to remain upright. Behind him, the grocery store glowed through the falling mist.

"Only guilty men know terror so profound," was the last thing the old man had said.

Chapter 24

When James got back to the house it was late. He knocked and after a time, Ellen let him in. In the dim light of the entry hall he could see something was wrong. At first, he was concerned about her head injury, but then he realized something else had happened. Getting home had used up the last of his strength. Dizziness was swarming in. The two of them went to the front room and sat.

"I went too far," Ellen said. She was twitching, glancing about the room. "There is a place you go, and you don't know how to get back."

"Sleep," James said. "It helps."

"I don't know how to get back," Ellen repeated, her voice trembling. James rose and went to where she was sitting. Her eyes were wide, darting about, as if she was looking at something too vast to take in. He sat a little apart from her.

"I've been where you are, many times," he said.

She was looking through him, but she made the slightest nod, yes.

"It is what happens sometimes. It won't stay this way," he said.

Ellen nodded yes again repeatedly, quick childlike movements. "I tell people that in my work," she said, seeing him for a split second, and then she was gone again.

"She was there. The girl I saw in the basement," Ellen said.

She pointed to the back of the house. She was struggling to slow it down, to recall the passing of events one individual moment at a time, to delay the cascade that threatened to overwhelm her.

"Then she was next to me," she said, gesturing with her hands a few inches apart to the place next to her. Her eyes registered shock after shock, her head jerking lightly each time. "She is in pain," Ellen whispered. "So much pain. So, so much …" Her voice trailed off. "I don't have …" Again, her voice trailed off. Blinking. "I can't …"

James took a deep breath. Exhaustion was clawing at him. Stars crept in along the edges of his vision. He put his hand out palm up.

"Ellen, take my hand," he said.

She looked at him, her lips working silently, as if seeing a stranger, suddenly too close.

"Ellen!" he said more loudly. "Take my hand."

She settled slightly, as if he was again visible to her. "This will hurt you."

"I'm more used to it," he said.

"I don't want to hurt you anymore," Ellen said.

"Take my hand," he repeated.

Her hand slowly rose off her lap. "I'm so sorry I fucked up again. I was arrogant. I had no idea," she whispered, and she took his hand.

Ellen woke with a start. The sun was pouring in. James was asleep on the far couch, his coat still on, snarled about him.

We're going to die here, she thought.

She rose and went up to the bathroom. When she returned, she found Jimmy awake. She studied him fumbling to get a cigarette

132

out of his pack. If he was aware of her, he did not look up.

"Another fucking day in paradise," he said. She crossed her arms, leaning against the door frame. Still not raising his head, he hooked his thumb toward the front door. "Buy me breakfast?"

She continued to study him, her arms remaining crossed.

"I'll tell you about my evening out," he said.

"Oh, yeah. How'd that go?" Ellen asked.

"Buy me breakfast and I'll tell you," he said.

She understood what he was doing. Getting her out. She gestured to the front door. "After you," she said.

The diner had booths. They sat, their heads down, eating. While a few customers near them conversed, James and Ellen did not. They had fallen into silence on the walk over and the silence held. Much like soldiers after a battle, trying to use words seemed a poor exchange. Their shared company was more eloquent.

As they ate in silence, each gauged how much damage they sensed in the other and in themselves. Expressions that came and went. A twitch. A small sound from the back of the throat. A hand rubbing a face. Lips pursing. When words finally came, they were simple.

"Thank you for looking after me," she said.

"Enlightened self-interest," he replied, looking up.

They sat on a park bench in the sun. It was a small city park on an anonymous block. They had arrived at it by simply wandering street by street, meandering under the blue sky. They sat for a time with their faces upturned to the sun. It is a common thing in cooler climates, when the sun makes an appearance, for people to sit and soak it in. You also see it outside hospitals.

Patients sitting in wheelchairs, their faces upturned. Some, in the last days of their lives, their faces upturned, the faintest of smiles.

Words exhausted; the sounds of the city flowed over them like water. There was the sound of a trolley bell a block up the hill. A passing car moving across. A radio somewhere above and over. A bird, two notes. A breeze moving among the leaves of a tree. A single bark from a dog. A question really.

"We need to compare notes," Ellen finally said.

James grunted. He looked at the buildings across the way. A fly landed on his cheek, then a second. She saw them swarming around him.

"Do you mind?" James asked. He held out his hand, palm up.

Ellen made it into a comical, grandiose gesture. She pointed her index finger, swept down from above and touched the tip of it to his open palm. The flies instantly disappeared.

"Why do they come after you as flies?" she asked.

"I guess we're further away from their source? I have no idea," James replied. "It's beyond me why they're so fond of you, but they keep coming after me," James said.

"We need to understand what's happening when we interact," Ellen replied.

"I don't get murdered by flies," James replied.

"Yes, but why?" Ellen responded. Then she faltered. "This is exhausting. It keeps piling up."

"All right, all right. I'm in," James replied, he shifted a bit toward her.

Ellen sat for a moment. "Look. May I ask you a personal question instead?" she said.

James turned his head a bit.

"Hm," he replied.

"You've always been alone?" she asked.

He turned and looked at her. "Where are you going with this?" he asked.

"I guess I want to understand the price. You've never had a relationship? No intimacy?" she finished.

He thought for a moment. "There are places downtown where you sit behind glass in booths. You put tokens in and watch," he said.

"To see women?" she asked.

"Those too I'm sure, but I watch men," he replied.

"Ah," she said. "But only behind glass."

"Yes, only behind glass," Jimmy replied. "Happy?"

She turned toward him, agitated.

"Everything was under control before all this started. Now it's gone. Everything I thought I knew is gone. Every assumption, my view of others, all of my endless judgments, even about you."

"I don't understand what purpose this serves for you," James said.

Ellen sat with it. "I just want to understand," she said.

"Ah. You want to know if you're going to have to pay the price I've been paying," James said, nodding. "I see."

"Is it so impossible for you to believe I care about you?"

James lit a cigarette and blew out a long plume of smoke. "Sorry. I'm not in the habit of being in ..." He waved his hand in a vague circle. "... conversations."

"No, I suppose not," Ellen said.

Time passed.

"My mother was obsessed with teaching me that the world isn't safe," he said. "For a while I fought against that idea. But over the years, I have learned the lesson enough times that I have come to agree with her. She knew what the world would do if it found out about me."

"She knew what you are?" Ellen said.

"My mother had the gift as well," James said. He shook his head. "Gift. Whoever named it that should be hung." His expression soured. "She figured out about me during a funeral when I was four years old. She hated me for it. Took her baby boy away from her, I guess. She made me pay every day for it."

"I'm so sorry, Jimmy," Ellen said. "We can stop," she added.

"This is the part I have never understood about shrinks. What possible value can there be to dredging up *this*?" he asked, holding his hands up. Ellen realized he was genuinely asking the question.

"Because, if you find someone to work with, you can move past the things that happened with your mother. How long has she been dead, Jimmy?"

"Forty years," he said.

"She's been gone for forty years. I'm just saying you can learn to let her go, Jimmy," Ellen replied.

"I said she was dead. I didn't say she was gone."

Ellen was staggered by statement. She flashed on her own mother. The implications of such a thing.

"Oh, God," she said. *I keep fucking up,* she thought. "Jimmy. I didn't mean to pry."

"It's all prying, Ellen. Every word spoken is prying."

And with that, it had all turned sour. For Ellen, the weight of more angry, unpredictable conflict with James became overwhelming. Her voice took on a pleading tone.

"Jimmy, you can say no to any question you want to," she said. "Jesus, Jimmy we could be dead any day now. If there is something you don't want to talk about just tell me no. But stop

136

treating me like I'm another one of them."

Jimmy turned to face her. "This thing right here, what we're doing? I would rather die than feel this," he said, stabbing his finger into his chest. "Are you listening, Ellen? Do you hear me, yet? Can we not do this, please? Fuck!"

Ellen gathered herself in, withdrawing. "Fine," she said under her breath.

They continued to sit. James took a few breaths. Time passed.

"What did you see when they dragged us down to the basement?" James asked. "From the beginning." His tone was neutral.

More time passed.

"I was dizzy at first," Ellen finally said. "Everything was a blur. When he finally let go of me, I saw the four of them. One of them had a gun. Then you were there next to me."

"What else?" he asked.

"It's not clear, but I recall seeing figures behind the men. Standing still," she said.

"How many?" James asked.

"Twenty or thirty. The basement was full. I took your hand."

"You knew what was going to happen?" James continued.

"It seemed like that was what would happen, yes," she replied.

"What were you feeling?"

Ellen closed her eyes for a moment. "Scared. Then very angry," she said. She turned and looked at James, a little surprised. "The figures, they came forward and attacked the men. Those men were on the floor screaming, bleeding, and I was laughing at them."

"Do you think you … made that happen?" James asked slowly.

Ellen sat quietly. A breeze stirred her hair. "I called to them for help." she replied.

"I'm beginning to think our gifts are very different," James said.

During the back and forth of the last few exchanges, Ellen's feeling of exhaustion had been offset by a rising hint of curiosity. *Come on curiosity,* she thought to herself, a hint of lightness rising in her.

"I've never had this before," James said. "A chance to compare the gift. How it operates."

Come on curiosity, Ellen thought for a second time.

James continued. "At first I was looking at those men, mostly at the one with the gun. I had no clear view of what was behind them until you took my hand. But then I saw hundreds of them. Extending back beyond the basement wall. Much further. Across the two yards, along the axis of the old hotel."

"I only saw the figures in the basement," Ellen replied.

"I think, you and me. We're a 'push me, pull you,'" James said.

"And what does that mean exactly?" Ellen replied.

"Last night I went somewhere," James said. "Somewhere I have not been since I was a child." He paused, collecting his thoughts. "This world. It's not just the living and dead. There are other things. I saw them on that night in Texas, and I guess I didn't really want to believe I would ever have to see them again, but ever since the activity has been increasing at the house? One of them has been trying to reach us," he said, looking out across the street.

"That's what you've been hiding from me," Ellen said.

"I just… I didn't want it to be happening," he replied.

"What is happening?" Ellen asked.

James rubbed his face. "You saw them in the basement, but I saw where they were coming from."

"You went there?" Ellen said.

"I did," James said.

There was a pause in the conversation. As if the weight of it needed to be shifted. Shouldered differently.

"Do we have an agreement, that you can just say no to any question you don't want to answer?" Ellen asked.

"That's always been the agreement," James said.

"Okay, but maybe we do the version where you don't me feel like shit." The slight pleading note was still there.

James sighed loudly. "Okay, okay. Fine. Whatever … no thank you," he said, emphasizing the last phrase.

Across the way the radio turned off. A siren passed far to the south. A bird, again just two notes. And just like that, the silences between them had become something new, an acknowledgement of their willingness to remain in each other's company regardless of how different they were.

"So," Ellen said, "You said your mother isn't gone. Is she here all the time …?"

"Mother fucker!" James said, turning to stare at Ellen. Even as she ducked her head away, he saw she had the slightest smile. He paused and took a breath. "Okay, okay, no, actually. Never, actually. She has only ever shown up when …" James fell silent. He put his head down on his hand.

"I'm so fucking blind," he said.

"What?" Ellen asked.

"She's on the porch," he said.

Chapter 25

"The devil you know," James said, smiling. He was sitting in the high-backed chair on the porch. Ellen stood leaning on the rail, looking at him.

"So now it doesn't bother you to sit here," Ellen asked.

"Not at all," he replied.

"Your mother, who has been dead for forty years, is on this porch, keeping it clear of whatever and you're okay with that," Ellen said. "Where exactly is she?" Ellen looked around the porch.

"Haven't the slightest idea," James replied.

"I see," Ellen said. "So, how do you know she's the one doing it?"

"The discomfort I was feeling before?" James replied. "It was familiar, but I wasn't making the connection."

"Familiar in what way?" she asked.

"Being kept safe. Her way of doing it," he said. "There's always an undercurrent of criticism and judgment. It's faint but it's here. She keeps the porch safe, and the price she extracts is her judgment."

"You're making me a little nervous, Jimmy. How are you arriving at all this?" Ellen asked.

"You agree that spirits are all around us?" James said.

"Yes," Ellen said.

"You also agree that a lot of people see them, yeah? But for the most part, they don't believe what they're seeing. Noticing spirits is like pulling on one end of that thread. Most people who get the slightest glimpse of them say, 'not real' and drop the thread. But those of us who hang on to the thread, we eventually see them. You see them first as shadows, impressions. Hang onto the thread longer and they become more solid. Hang on long enough and what they're feeling becomes real to us. But each one is its own thread. I have all these threads I've been holding, but my mother? Now I'm holding that one."

"But you can't see her," Ellen said.

"Not yet," he said.

"Why?" Ellen asked.

"She has been gone a long time, I guess" he replied.

"And you're still angry at her," Ellen said.

"Oh, yes," he replied, smiling.

"But you're okay sitting on the porch."

"It's damned peaceful," James said. "Now that I know why."

James looked over his shoulder into the front room.

"Maybe we get her somewhere to sit," James said.

Ellen went into the house. She felt dizzy and confused. Like something was draining her focus, her ability to understand or make sense. She took a chair from the dining room and walked back up the hall. As she got closer to the porch, she felt nauseous. It was all cascading. She was struggling to slow it down. She went back out onto the porch and put the chair down next to Jimmy. Then she went back to leaning on the rail, her arms crossed, defensive. Something was aggravating her sense of threat. And then James spoke.

"Hm," James said. "Do you see anything sitting on the rail, right there?" He pointed to a spot a few feet to Ellen's right. Ellen unclasped her arms and stepped slowly to her left.

"What the fuck, Jimmy. No, I don't see anything," she said alarmed.

"Hm," Jimmy replied.

Ellen moved further to her left, rotating to stand near Jimmy.

"You should probably see this," James said, holding out his hand. Ellen paused for a moment, then she took his hand.

"Mother fucker!" Ellen barked out. The crow stood before her on the rail. It spread its wings partially and then, shaking out its feathers, settled.

"What do I have to do to convince you I'm fucking overwhelmed, Jimmy?" She flung Jimmy's hand away. "What the fuck is wrong with you?" The crow remained before her. Something about the creature made her skin crawl in the most obscene way. "No, no, no ..." she said under her breath.

"I told you when big events happen it attracts attention. We have attracted the attention of something," James said. "This is its calling card."

Ellen began to shudder. "Something's wrong," Ellen muttered. The crow turned its head to one side, the endless gulf of its black eyes reflecting nothing. A chill reached up from Ellen's gut, a cold hand taking hold of her heart. A sense of deep despair began to steal over her, her blood slowing.

"Okay, okay," James said, rising and stepping in front of Ellen. "That's enough of that," he said to the crow. "I'll call you when I'm ready for another chat."

The crow cocked its head.

"I said I'll let you know, now piss off!" James said in a loud voice. The crow rose on lazy wings and wheeled out and away across the street. It settled on the porch across the way.

"This thing, you went to visit it?" Ellen asked, shocked.

"I did," James replied.

"Jesus, Jimmy," she realized she was two steps back, pressing against the windows. "Why would you do that?"

"Why did you call the girl to you?"

"Because I was an idiot," Ellen replied angrily.

"Well, there you have it," Jimmy responded. "We're idiots."

James sat smoking as the afternoon light shifted toward a golden glow. Ellen had called for take-out food. Now she sat on the front step. A dark mood had crept over her. The thing she had seen on her porch unnerved her deeply. The ease with which James had made the decision to reveal it to her felt invasive. She was struggling not to conflate him with it. *What if he is not what he pretends to be?* she thought. Ellen understood that he had done what she had demanded he do. He had revealed to her what he was hiding. But she was wholly unprepared for this terrible despair that had swarmed over her. Comprehending the presence of Jimmy's mother was one thing. Seeing the crow was like falling into a well. The lurching sensation of a headlong pitch in and down, knowing that somewhere in the blackness below, rushing up, was the ugly finality of it.

Then Ellen thought of a colleague from years ago, an older woman who had worked for decades in the battered women's center where Ellen had interned.

"We see a lot of terrible things in this work," the woman had once said. "You can't avoid it. What I have decided is that it's my responsibility to keep my vibrations up," the woman had said, even as she rose to go see her next client, a fourteen-year-old rape survivor. The child's mother had allowed her boyfriend access to the girl for years. In her mind's eye, Ellen could still see the therapist, her figure upright and resolute, escorting the girl into her office all those years ago, a picture of wildflowers half visible on the wall inside, the door swinging gently shut. Ellen took a breath and closed her eyes.

Eventually James spoke again.

"When I looked down the line of figures in the basement out along the axis of the hotel? I saw something at the back or felt it. Something like this one." He gestured across the street. "Maybe they come in pairs," James said.

"Why didn't you warn me?" she said. "You just all of a sudden show me that?"

"I'm sorry," he said. "I don't really understand how other people will react. I don't have much practice understanding people actually," He shrugged. "Once it found me, I knew it was a matter of time until it found you. You had to be warned," James answered. "My guess is they're something very old, something from nature. One is down there." He pointed towards the basement behind him. "And this one," he gestured across the street, "is drawn to it."

A man across the street, raised his phone and took a photo of the house. James stood. "Excuse me," he said. He started down the steps and the man began quickly walking away. When he turned back, Ellen had gone inside. James followed her into the house. He found her upstairs, packing a bag. He remained in the hall.

"Where will you go?" he asked.

"I don't know, but I can't stay here," she replied. She was in a panic, stuffing things into a small carrying bag. "I'm not going to die in this fucking place."

"Can't say as I blame you for wanting to run away," James

replied.

Ellen stormed past him and headed down the stairs. He followed, but slowly. When he reached the front door, it was wide open. Ellen was sitting on the top step, her bag flung into the middle of the yard. She was weeping tears of rage and grief.

James sat down next to her. "You should probably tell me about the girl," he said. "But first, you need to pay the delivery guy." A man stood at the gate with a bag of Chinese take-out, his eyes wide. Ellen nodded yes and walked down the steps, wiping her nose on her sleeve. She took some bills out of her pocket and paid for the food, returning up the steps to sit. She handed one of the orders to James and opened the other for herself. She carefully opened a packet of soy sauce, poured it on the food and began methodically eating. When the food was gone, she set the take-out box on the step next to her.

"Feel better?" James asked.

"I do feel a little better," she replied.

Ellen rose and walked back down the steps to where her bag lay in the yard. She picked it up. For a moment, she stood looking up at the house, then with the tiniest shake of her head, she walked back up the steps. She stopped next to James. "The girl. She's begging me to help her. She's begging," Ellen said, tears running slowly down her face. "And I honestly don't think I can even go near her again." Then she went into the house to put her bag away.

As James watched her go, an idea arrived. *I'm going to have to teach her*, he thought. A range of emotions rose. For a child who had grown up abandoned to no understanding, no sense making, abandoned to finding his own way amidst terrors, the realization that he might teach her, was directly in contrast to his long history of isolation.

146

"What you never did for me," he said aloud. A chill rolled across the porch. He laughed, scoffing. "One hell of a job, too."

The quiet on the porch was giving James an opportunity to hear himself think. What came to him was the degree to which his thoughts had always been a muddy synthesis of his ideas and the thoughts of the dead swarming in, always intruding.

He was also hearing himself because of Ellen, in the back and forth of their talking. Surprisingly, that back and forth was growing his willingness to take risks. Risks not only on his own behalf, but also for her. It was an odd sensation, familiar, long forgotten.

Ellen sat in her father's room on the hospital bed, her head down, her palms upturned in her lap. She thought back to the long days and nights when her father had lain there, one man doing the work of preparing to die. For her, being witness to this process had been silence itself. She had quickly come to understand that her words, her issues were simply not part of it. He only ever asked for someone, anyone, to help with his biological needs until, one by one, each of those finally quieted and ceased. And despite the slow ticking of the clock, stretching over days, weeks, months, sometimes years, they do end. She remembered her little internal gasp of surprise at the simple sentence, "He is unable to swallow water anymore."

The experience of being there in the long nights of silence alongside him had, despite her best efforts, amplified the jangling calliope of her resentments toward him, dwarfed as they were alongside the immensity of his dying. She had decided it was some smallness in her nature that kept them present. Because her resentments would not go, they seemed to her to become brittle, trivial; followed by the seduction to believe that all of who we are is brittle, trivial.

She had never before been a primary care giver to a dying person. The hospice workers who came each day, who had witnessed hundreds of such events, offered some insights including, "Don't take his silence personally, he's just doing his work."

Small comfort that, as the same thing could be said of him for all the years she had spent as a child in his house. As a recovering alcoholic, his was a fierce determination to not fall back into drinking, but also to keep at bay shame, regret, secrets he did not want to share. He never spoke of any of it. What did he say at his meetings? Who had he been when he raged in the bars? What thoughts passed through his head as he was facing the end of his life? All a mystery kept locked away. It was just a few days ago she had finally come to understand that her own self isolation was mirrored back by his. Arriving at that understanding was enough to let him go, if not forgive him.

And now he was gone. No whisper of him remained. She felt a pang of loss, if not for him, for the person she was when she had cared for him. The days during which he lay dying seemed like years ago. Who she had been sitting beside his bed, now also gone, her long-held judgments evaporated, the bottom having fallen out of her understandings of the world.

What she had not told James was that the girl's presence was pulling at her now. Very lightly calling her down to the basement. It was a consistent tug at her consciousness. A tone in the background of everything. The shock of that child's immense physical pain had dropped into her body and remained, emanating reverberations of despair. *I can't find my way back,* she thought, *to before this.* Even if only back to the long nights during the decline of her father, much less the life she had led before he fell ill.

Then, a memory, a small shock of recognition, and the realization blossomed. It wasn't that she couldn't go back. Quite the contrary, the girl's pleading for help, her pain and despair was calling Ellen to something much further back. A child in a diner sitting before her long-finished breakfast plate, her mother next to her talking raucously and loudly to a man she did not know, empty beer bottles filling the table.

No, she thought, tears starting again. She was collapsing.

As a therapist, learning to keep a safe degree of separation from her clients' emotions was what allowed her to hear even the most terrible of stories and not collapse into them. Such stories were rare in her current practice. Most of her clients were people of means who struggled with the daily challenges born out of wealth or position that they could not untangle. One day, she might be helping a couple, their wedding fast approaching, work through a prenuptial agreement where millions of dollars were at stake. Another day, she might be helping parents struggling with the challenges of their dysfunctional parenting, their children venting out their anger as strident disrespect or sullen surrender.

But there were always moments, which client or what context could never be predicted, when the darkest of human stories would suddenly emerge. A story of an interaction, perhaps long ago, perhaps yesterday, when a human being is savagely brutalized or is revealed to have committed such an act, and she, as a therapist, must hold space for it. When working in shelters or hospitals, it could be a daily challenge. Because of this, therapists must learn to keep themselves separate from the emotional impact of other's trauma, to not collapse into it, even when clients sometimes turn their rage directly on the therapist. Never collapse into the trauma.

Remain separate. Be still and calm.

When she had invited the girl from the basement to sit with her, those well-trained barriers of emotional distance so carefully constructed, her secure scaffoldings of identity, were breached in an instant. The girl had come gently, tentatively, as children will do, a silhouette containing a gulf of endless shadow, utterly empty, reflecting nothing. And in the moment of contact, her pain, immense beyond all possibility had collapsed Ellen's defenses, gone in the first flicker of contact, shattered. Not only between her and the girl's terrible history, but also another.

Sitting in her father's room, sunlight streaming in, grief engulfing her, she had yet to realize what had happened. What her surging fear already knew, she did not yet realize. The ultimate source of her overwhelming grief. A child was indeed calling out to her, desperately begging for help, trapped in a place it could not escape, a child she had locked away, silenced all the years of her adult life.

James started up the stairs to where Ellen sat in her father's room. Hearing that she was crying, he paused, turning to sit on the stairs halfway up. He noted that the second floor of the house was clear. Ellen's father was gone. That departure had removed a level of confusion the place had been creating, discordant notes. Now, only one note remained from down below in the basement. That terrible note was surging, but the porch and the upstairs now represented little safe harbors of order in the chaos of the house. They would collapse, more likely sooner than later, but for the first time it occurred to James that such frail and transitory order was what humans can offer each other. That within such refuges, anger, rage, grief, and loss are calmed, that they abate, lessen.

150

For the first time in a long time, James thought of his own father, sitting at the dinner table night after night. James and his mother flailing at each other, vindictive and resentful combatants locked in a mutual stranglehold as the dead swarmed about them.

His father, seated nightly at that table, sometimes averting his eyes, occasionally raising his voice in anger to quiet the endless turmoil. That his father spent his nights sleeping alongside a woman with the gift, a woman tormented by it, was suddenly unfathomable to James. His father, pedantically asserting his middle-class illusion of order, without which they likely would have spun apart and been swallowed by the chaos they themselves were formed out of. Without that lonely, stoic man they might have simply gone mad.

And what of his mother, the last remnants of her grim determination still out there on the porch, holding the line against those like her? It was not really her. Even when she first had returned, moonlight spilling across the white of her funeral dress in the dark woods of Texas all those years ago, she had been only partially there. A thing of rigid purpose, the warmth of her, such as it was, vanished and gone. The urge to protect her son, so strong in life, had lived on past her dying. While still among the living, she would have done better to teach him, not suppress him, but teaching was, for her, to reinforce that he obey, mind, do as he was told, be invisible. It was no formula to prepare any child for the horrors of the world, just a desperate ploy to stave off tomorrow, daily.

James took a deep breath. He rose and continued to the top of the stairs. He heard Ellen shifting now, his steps audible on the creaking stairs. He arrived at the door to the old man's room and tapped lightly on the doorframe.

She looked up; her expression lost and innocent, her eyes wide in wonder. Her mouth was moving with the beginnings of half-formed questions, but she did not look away. Something was there that made common meaning between them, and she was arriving at it. It was coming to her, just as surely as he had come up the stairs, and she need only look at him for it to completely arrive.

"You and I," she said.

He smiled, his head bobbing lightly, an emotion he could not hope to name, there in his chest.

She was smiling, tears still running down her face. "I'm the crier, I guess," she said.

"Yeah," he replied.

"We are not so different," she said. "I'm a therapist and I have no idea how to accept help, how to even ask for it," she said. And then she began laughing. Her sparkling laughter rose in the room and danced off the sunny windows. It echoed up and down the hallway, bounding down through the house, stirring the shadows in the basement in unforeseen ways.

James saw his own father at the dinner table, laughing on one of the rare nights when the conflicts were quieted, and some small mutual connection had arrived for the three of them.

"And I'm a drunk who won't drink," he said.

"You're a lot more than that," she replied. "You're a walking miracle, Jimmy. You're brave and kind and powerful and reliable." She wiped her eyes and took a deep breath. "And so am I," she said, the last of her tears falling down her face.

After a moment, she spoke half to herself, half to him. "What are we so scared of? What have we always been so scared of?"

They fell silent for a while.

"I was sixteen years old when they strapped me down on the

electroshock table," he said. "This one shrink had fooled me into thinking he understood; that he got me. He suckered me in. Built that trust. He sat there making his notes with those warm eyes. I guess I had a crush on him. I think maybe he knew that and used it. I started telling him some of the things I was seeing. Some of the things I knew. Never once did he indicate he was anything but okay with what I was saying. After eight months of talk, sometimes twice a day, he closed up his notebook, wrote his report and off I want to electroshock. Guess he thought I was too far gone for more medication or talk therapy," Jimmy said, smiling ruefully.

"When they strapped me down, he was there. My last fucking hope, standing right there at the end of the table. I struggled like crazy. In the very last minutes I thought he might somehow, in some way, get me out of it. They put that wooden dowel in my mouth, held my head, and still I was thrashing. And then, right before the juice hit, I stopped struggling. Once I said, I don't expect to survive this, once I said, I don't expect anyone to come to help, once I said, fuck it, it got peaceful."

"God, Jimmy," she said.

"I never told another shrink a word. Not a fucking word. But that version of me on the table. He stayed. He knew what it takes to make it through. When the crow came and all the fear came with it, my sixteen-year-old self walked right back into the room," James said. "I didn't expect him. Didn't even realize he was an option, but there he was. What's so nice about him? Once you don't expect to survive, you can let go of all those calculations and just figure out how to do some damage. And if you think about it, we can do some damage, Ellen. Not to those poor souls in the basement, but to whatever is behind them, keeping them here. That thing. I've seen its kind before." James leaned forward, "Its kind can be hurt. I've seen it done. Hell, Ellen, I'm the one who did it."

"That's why you went to see the crow," Ellen said.

"To see if I could hold my own," James said.

"And how did that go?" Ellen asked.

"Not bad. It seems confused. Like it doesn't have any more clarity than we do," James said. "At least not that one. I think we can get it to do what we want."

"Jesus, Jimmy, what if it's listening?" Ellen said.

"I hope it is," Jimmy replied. "I don't intend to trick it. I'm going to make a deal with it."

"Is that safe?" Ellen said.

"At this point? … Fuck it." James said, making a comical flourish.

Ellen sat for a moment. "What about that psychiatrist?"

James smiled. "Mom took an interest in him. He came to me a week or so later, just before he quit his job and left. Said he was sorry. Said he had no idea. Begged me to make it stop, that kind of thing. Serves him right if he got the dowel in his mouth at some point. I told him that she wasn't going to listen to me. I said, he could have, but she wasn't going to. She has a vindictive streak a mile wide."

"How often did she do that?" Ellen asked.

"You mean attach herself to someone?" he replied.

"Like that," Ellen said.

"Almost never. I didn't see her after that for a very long time," he said.

Ellen thought for a moment. "I think what happened to the psychiatrist? That's happened to me," she said. "The girl from the basement. She's there now. All the time." Ellen gestured with her open hand toward the side of her head. "She's calling. All the time.

154

I don't know what I'm going to do."

James took a long breath. "I see," he said. He shifted his weight. "We use it," he finally said.

Ellen grimaced.

"I know, I know, but listen to me," James said. "There's always a key. If there's only one entity, then the key is obvious. If there is more than one, the key eventually comes forward. In this case, she's the one coming forward, multiple times. She reached out to me. Which is very odd, given the general mood in the basement. If she's the key, then she's the one keeping the rest here."

"She's forcing them to stay?"

"No, she's being used to do it. The crow's counterpart? That is forcing them to stay, but it's using her to do it."

"So what do we do?" Ellen asked.

"Hm," James said. "Yeah, that's the part you're not going to like."

"Maybe not today, okay?" she said.

"Yeah, maybe not today," he replied.

Chapter 26

The sun rose and they rose with it. They spent the morning doing nothing, simple things, letting the time pass mostly without comment. Eating sandwiches a block from Ellen's home. Standing out front of the house for sale around the corner. Musing.

At one point, James found himself sitting in a solitary chair in a dress shop on Market Street. People outside flowing past on the wide sidewalks. He had a cup of coffee in his hand. Across from him, Ellen moved her hand along the rack of clothing, lifting out items as they caught her attention. The dress shop specialized in imported linen blouses and skirts, dyed in bright jewel tones, flurries of color in the front window that shifted with the seasons.

Ellen had two blouses already hanging across her arm. James sat watching her as she slowly passed back and forth before him. It was a curious sensation, the simplicity of the moment coupled with the fact that he had never in his life sat in a chair like this, watching someone shop.

"I pass this place all the time and I always say I should go in, but I never do," Ellen said. She looked at a bright yellow blouse and returned it to the rack. A fly could be seen circling near James, then another. She circled past James, high fiving him lightly without even a glance down as she passed. A young women smiled from behind the sales counter having no idea of what had just transpired.

Ellen stopped at a display of silver earrings near the register. It was a costume jewelry, a rainbow of bright glass beads. Ellen held up a pair alongside her face, turning to one side and then the other before a small mirror. She put the earrings and the blouses in the counter.

After a while longer, she made her purchases, and they left the store. As they walked along the busy street, she lifted the shopping bag slightly and said, "This is what I'm going to wear when this is all over."

Not long after, Ellen found herself sitting in her front room watching Jimmy as he slept, splayed out on the couch across from her. He had come in after lunch and promptly laid down to sleep, not acknowledging to her he was even planning to do so, drifting off in minutes. It was a reminder of his lack of social awareness, born out of a lifetime of isolation. His breathing was regular, no catches or murmurs that might suggest troubling dreams.

It occurred to her that James had probably not slept with another person watching over him for decades. Which was why the book she had been reading was now face down in her lap and had been for some time.

So much of Ellen's experience of James was his outsized personality, his sometimes-aggravating ways of expressing himself, his unpredictable reactivity. Only in sleep could she examine his face still and calm, undistracted by his scowling, or laughter, or worry. In the peace of sleep, she could see the boy in him, the older man's careworn face relaxing to let the child show itself. She had noticed a few days back that when James slept, the flies did not come. A curious thing. Are we somewhere else when we're dreaming? she thought. Are we, in fact, *dead to the world?*

Next to Ellen on the side table, sitting stiff and upright, was the paper shopping bag which held her new clothes. The store's logo was an abstract butterfly printed in maroon ink, created years ago, an aspirational moment in someone's life. How many years back had they poured over ideas, creating this little piece of the world. Five years? Ten? Comparing paper stocks, printing up labels, business cards, stickers, considering illuminated signage and then thinking better of it.

To this day, out into the city these bags wandered, holding items wrapped in crepe paper, a note about a sale tucked in amidst the riot of colored fabrics. The bag is emptied, finds its way to the trash. The shirts are hung up, worn. Someday, an accidental stain happens that won't come out. Someday, they aren't the right style, don't feel fresh or new, no longer flatter an aging body. One only ever, was engulfed in a roaring house fire, bright fabric waving frantically in the updraft. But eventually, it's all gone, like the billions of little worlds that came before it, back down the ages to hearths tended and trails walked from the very beginning. The story of us all. Little worlds vanished.

And yet, there sat the shopping bag, upright, like a small paper soldier. Bravely standing its ground, this little world someone had created.

James sat up, rubbing his face. She rose and put her book back on the bookshelf. They looked at each other, she giving him time to shake off sleep, return to the world. After a few moments, he turned his head slightly to one side and raised his eyebrows.

She shrugged.

"Then I guess we should get started," he said.

Chapter 27

They sat on the front porch, side by side in two chairs. A few cars passed, but the street was quiet; a midafternoon lull. James extended his hand to Ellen. A cold breeze swept across them.

"Ma …" James said. "Settle down." He cocked his head sideways, listening. "Well, it's a shame you're not running things anymore," he said.

Ellen shook her head in small quick movements, keeping her eyes down. "Can you see her?" she asked.

"Just a shadow of her," James replied.

"Well, that's great. Just great. Okay," Ellen whispered. She gathered herself, sitting up straight and took James' hand. James looked out at the house across the street.

"Come on, then," he said.

A supreme stillness settled over the street. As if the world had decided to pause its mad trembling for one brief moment. Then the crow's wings swept up and it settled on the rail.

"Is she for me?" a voice said from somewhere above them, damp cold stone.

"You want company or not?" James replied.

"I suppose," the voice said, the gentle tug of the grave.

"Then quit fucking around," James replied.

The crow tipped its head. "Chatty insect," the voice replied.

"I'll be back," James said to Ellen. "Don't let go of my hand."

The old man sat across from James at his great desk, his eyes glowing with malice. James felt Ellen's hand in his but there was no one beside him. "Hm," he said. He turned to the old man. "I'm here to trade."

The old man smiled, creating red, bloody cracks in the flesh of his face, if it even was flesh. "There are seven sins that whet the appetite of my kind. You have already committed two of them. Which means I can peel off two layers of what protects you. So, I'm going to do that now, if you don't mind," the old man said.

"Are threats the best you can offer by way of conversation?" James said. He felt a shift in the room. The old man was closer to him somehow. The desk was smaller?

"I have your information for you," the old man said. "You ask your little question, and I will tell you what you want to know. But I'll not be tricked this time. This time, I want something in return." He smiled, his face cracking, small rivulets of blood working their way downward.

"What do you want?" James asked.

"I want to see that basement," the old man said.

"Why?" James responded.

"Is that your question?" the old man asked, his head cocking sideways.

"No, that's not my question," James replied. "Why do you want to see the basement?"

The old man pursed his lips. Drops of blood followed the outlines of his mouth before continuing down his chin. His tongue darted out for a moment.

"I have business there," the old man said.

"Ah, business," James replied. "Now business I can do."

162

"What do you know of it?" the old man asked.

"I know you want out of here," James replied. "You stink of it."

The old man was gone. Something infinite filled the space beyond the desk, a stirring of the charnel house, a thing of vast starvation, beyond all hungers, languidly moving in and out of existence before him. A voice spoke, the cracking of tree limbs in winter.

"The first sin is to deceive; the second sin is hubris" The desk was gone. The thing was close now.

"You can sit in my lap for all I care," James said. "Are you going to ask me what I have to offer?"

"I know what you have to offer, little tastes of deception and hubris from an insect whose time in the world is less than a wink. A trifling. When I was first abroad in the world, your kind had barely washed up on the shore, gasping for water, gulping air, neither ever good enough. That has not changed. Nothing ever good enough until darkness comes and then the begging starts," the voice said.

"I'll show you the basement," James said.

"In exchange for your question," it replied.

"In exchange for my question," James said.

"An outright lie," the thing said. "Your third sin." There was a pause, the air shimmered. The old man was again there, behind his great desk. His demeanor mild, even apologetic. "Not a lie," he said.

"No," James said. "Not a lie."

"I wonder," the old man said. "What is the end of you, exactly?"

"Your business in the basement. It is with another of your

kind, yeah?" James said.

The old man drew back. He cocked his head sideways. "You have a mark on you."

James held up his free left hand. There was a wound in the center of his palm. The head of a cloisonné pin in the form of jeweled flowers, flickered there. "This place brings out the best in me."

The crow rose up behind the old man on top of the chair. It spread its wings, blotting out the library behind it in shadow. A threat. Then, oddly, something rose behind James. Something equal and opposite.

"A word of advice," the old man said.

"Yeah?" James said.

"Don't look behind you, you're not ready yet," the old man said. The crow dropped its wings and settled, diminished. The old man bobbing his head apologetically.

James noticed he was not feeling the deep exhaustion that had crept up on him before. Increasing stamina? Ellen's hand in his?

The old man licked his lips, his tongue darting about. "Gold and men. They become … so wretched and delicious. I let myself fall into some distasteful habits. You of all people should understand how that feels," he said.

"Not the same," James replied. "Another of your kind, yeah?"

The old man looked distressed. He slowly swung his head side to side. "A delicate matter. Things out of balance. Appetites that overwhelm and subjugate. We can gorge ourselves, become weighed down, stranded." He took on a wistful quality.

James reached out and took a small object off the desk. The old man watched him and sighed. "There was a time when such things would have ruptured the world. Now you just take my things," he said.

"You love it," James replied, smiling.

"How?" the old man asked.

"How long has it been since you've seen anything new?" James asked him.

The old man bobbed his head. "Don't take anything else."

"I'll get back to you on that." James smiled. "So, about my question."

"The Hotel Empress," the old man said.

"What was it at the start?" James asked.

"And you will show me the basement," the old man said, his eyes betraying such appetite.

"That is the agreement," James said.

James was back on the porch with Ellen. He released her hand.

"Are you going?" she asked.

"Already went," he said.

"You just now said don't let go of my hand and then you dopped my hand," she replied, confused.

"Hm. No time passes," James replied. "Because I was there for a while."

"No time passes. Great. What am I supposed to do with that?" she muttered looking at her hand.

James cracked his knuckles. "I have to say, it went better than I expected."

"Something *is* different," Ellen said.

"Yes, I think you were there with me," he said. "Or some part of you."

Ellen looked about her. "The crow is gone. But it's not gone …" she said, her voice trailing off. "And the hotel?" she asked.

"Before they dragged it up on shore, it was called *La Emperatriz*." James replied.

"A sailing ship," she said.

"They didn't have enough storage or housing during the height of the gold rush, so, they dragged abandoned ships up on shore. Hundreds are buried under the city, all around us," he said, gesturing.

"And what deal did you make to get that bit of information?" Ellen asked.

"I agreed to show it the basement," James replied. "What I didn't say was when."

"Do you think that's smart? To keep messing with it like that?" she asked.

James turned to face her. "You have the ability to call into this world those spirits that you hold threads to," James said. "It is one of the ways we can do damage."

"So, you showed me to him," she said.

"I don't know if the same rules apply to something like the crow, but it knows who you are, and it understands you're … not on the menu. Assuming I can keep the upper hand."

James looked down at his left hand, still tightly closed. He opened his fingers. "Well, fuck me," he said under his breath. There in his palm was a small carved stone, an Egyptian scarab. He sighed, gathering himself.

"Okay, well it looks like I brought this back. Which makes it a very powerful object," James said, holding the scarab up. "It's a bridge to where the crow is trapped."

Ellen put her hand out, but James drew his back. "You shouldn't touch it. Not unless you absolutely have to," he said.

"Why?" Ellen asked.

"It will change you," James replied.

"So, how has it changed you?" she asked.

"The first time I touched something like this? I lost my mind," James replied.

"Jimmy, this isn't very helpful. I don't know what you want me to do. All you seem to do is warn me off things. Or make cryptic comments," Ellen said.

"Okay, okay," James said putting the scarab in his pocket. "You want to try?"

"Try what?" Ellen replied.

"Try to call the crow here," James said. "Not all the way here, just reach out and connect. Just a bit."

Ellen drew back. "I'm not getting anywhere near that thing," she said, her voice rising.

"You asked," James replied.

Ellen fell silent, her heart racing. "All of this is royally fucked up," she finally said.

"Well, we either do something or we wait around for something to be done to us," James replied. "You think I'm not scared?" James rose and put his hand on the glass of the window. Flies swarmed on the inside of the glass, making a boiling mass of insects. The mass of flies grew larger than his hand. An audible angry buzz could be heard vibrating the glass. "This is a lot worse than it was a few days ago. If I don't figure out how to clear the basement, I won't be able to run far enough. This is how I'm going to die in some goddamn hotel in Sacramento."

Ellen rose slowly and stood next to him. She put her hand on the glass, but no insects came to where her hand was. She looked at him, her expression puzzled. She was reminded of the client that nearly attacked her years ago. A domestic abuser who didn't like the line of questioning she was presenting to him. *Why is this any more frightening?* she thought. She felt her legs nearly giving way beneath her. Just like then. She felt her pulse racing. Just like then. She felt a sense of the unfairness of it all. That violence was the way of the world. Just like then.

"Fuck it," she said, her temper rising. "Tell me what to do," she said.

"I'm not sure I know. This part is your thing, calling them." James took his hand off the window and returned to his chair. "I guess you just try to do it, intentionally."

Ellen walked back to stand by the railing. She took a deep breath. "I'm just going to picture the crow, just that bird, and see if I can call it here."

"Okay," James said.

Ellen closed her eyes. She pictured the crow on the railing. "Come," she said softly.

James looked over his shoulder. "Great, now mother is here," he said, rolling his eyes.

Then James was knocked sideways out of the chair. He rolled and came to a brutal halt against the porch railing. Ellen rushed to where he lay. James was wide-eyed with shock. A hard crosswind erupted on the porch, rattling the windows for a moment.

James sat up, staring, his hand out in front of him. "Ma! Shut up!" he yelled. It was the voice of a child's sudden, absolute terror. He turned to Ellen, not seeing her. "You didn't call the crow. You called the other one!" Then he screamed and was knocked sideways again.

Ellen scrambled to where he was and grabbed his hand; a wave of suffocation swarming over her – James' eyes staring up, contact with him accelerating the fear she had only just been

168

gaining a foothold against. She flung his hand away, scrambling backwards until she collapsed in a heap. Something ancient and cold had touched her ever so lightly. The lightest of contacts and she was down, unable to help James, unable to rise, unable to breathe.

James struggled to move, collapsed and struggled to rise again. He crawled inch by inch toward Ellen, pointing to the window to her left. A cold wind rose, hammering the windows. His eyes aglow, insistent, he pointed again.

Ellen felt another wave of terror rising and broke eye contact, turning purely by accident toward the window he was indicating. And there she was, just beyond the glass, the girl from the basement. Ellen forced herself to keep looking.

I do this or I die here, she realized. She pushed up onto her forearms, rising toward the glass. There was the girl's face, features beginning to emerge from the silhouette. Ellen raised her hand to the glass and the girl began to raise hers. The hand hung tentative in the air a few inches off the other side of the glass. The next wave of terror hit Ellen, vast and unrelenting. It was deep water, no light, no color, no sound; with crushing weight, water so deep and silent and dark that she was entombed in suffocation, in silence, and then, suddenly angry. *So very angry at not being allowed to sleep.* Then, she saw no more.

Chapter 28

James lay for a time seemingly unconscious, gently reaching out along the shattered avenues of his senses. Tentatively trying the smallest instance of listening, ready to withdraw into catatonia should the great, terrible hand descend on him again. It was a level of fear he had not previously experienced. To experience existing in any way was now a terror. An existential jump scare at every level of perception. It took an age for him to decide that listening was perhaps safe. Perhaps. He wondered about Ellen, his mother, the house, the trees in the side yard, now so completely separate from him, perceptions of which were cut off entirely by some lizard brain default switch. What sense might he try next? Touch? No. Smell? No. Sight? No.

I have to get away. And with that he found himself in the crow's library, sitting before the great desk. The room was empty, the books towering overhead. James felt the terror on the porch now distinctly separate from him, muted. For a time he rested, collecting himself. The temptation to stay was powerful. A day? A week? A hundred years? What harm could it do?

"Fuck it," he muttered, and the library was gone. James rose and knelt over Ellen. While he had taken time to recover in the library, not a single second had passed on the porch. Ellen was unconscious.

He felt a strange disassociation between the relative calm of his mind and the shocks of trauma that were continuing to move in waves through his body. He stumbled to the rail of the porch and vomited. He looked up at a family of four passing on the sidewalk, two children openly staring at him. He waved, half bent over, wiping his mouth with his other hand. They hurried on, herded along by their parents. "Now there's some next level fucking parenting," he muttered.

He returned to Ellen, and sat heavily next to her, putting his head in his hands. He fished in his pocket for a cigarette, lit it and sat with the tremors moving through in his body. "Did not see that coming," he said. He raised his head, listening, impatient. "Yeah, sometimes I should listen to you, Ma."

He reached out toward Ellen and then withdrew his hand, trembling. His expression hardened and he took Ellen's hand in his. He sat bolt upright as the impact of their shared perceptions intermingled, sending waves of shocks through him. He held his own against the spiking panic. "Come on, Ellen, come back to me."

Ellen was not moving. He feared some deeper damage had been done. That Ellen no longer had any reason now to return. *I have to get her away from here.*

Again, he found himself in the crow's library sitting before the great desk, but this time he was not alone. There, next to him, sat Ellen, her hand in his. She looked slowly about at the shelves of books disappearing into the murk above.

The old man sat on the other side of the desk. It was smiling, blood dripping off its chin. The crow was perched above it on the top of its tall chair.

"You certainly know how to make a bad situation worse. I'll give you that," the old man said.

172

"She was on the other side of the window," Ellen said to James, her tone puzzled.

The old man looked at her, startled, suddenly seeing her for the first time, its head turning side to side, like an animal trying to judge distance. It began to speak. Then stopped. Again it started to say something and again it stopped.

"She needed a place to rest," James said to the old man, gesturing to Ellen.

The old man continued to turn its head side to side. The crow began dancing nervously.

"Deceiver," the old man finally said. "A place to rest? She'll dissipate here. Be gone to dust."

"The last time we spoke, you came to understand that I could bring you to the basement, yeah?" James said.

The old man looked more closely at Ellen.

"Another deceiver," the old man said.

"This is where the crow is trapped?" Ellen said, shaking off her drowsiness.

The old man was gone in an instant, his great chair empty.

James looked at her. "Yeah, this is it."

"I feel different here. It's calm," she said. Ellen looked at her hand and arm. "So, we're what? In the afterlife or…?"

"Hm," James replied with a shrug. "For the time being, better not let go of my hand."

"Okay … Why am I here?" she said, still half in a dream.

"I brought you to rest. I shouldn't have asked you to call the crow. But here, we can step away from what's happening. We can collect our thoughts."

"Time doesn't pass here?" Ellen said, her eyes wide.

"Not as far as I can tell," James replied.

"What happened, when I tried to call the crow?" Ellen said.

"You called the other one. The one I saw in the basement," James said.

"Ridiculous," the old man said suddenly back in his chair. "She could no sooner call that one than raise the dead back to life."

"Don't talk about me like I'm not here," Ellen said.

The old man was gone again.

James drummed his fingers on the desktop. "I'm going to take some more of your stuff," he said to the empty air above them.

The old man was back at the desk. "Hidden so very well," he said. "Two deceivers, obscuring their natures, invoking disruption and disturbing the order of things, all the while hiding their true natures from each other." He turned and addressed Ellen directly, a smile curling along his lips. "Is there anyone you don't lie to?"

Ellen set her jaw, leaning forward.

"I've come to trade," James said.

"Ha!" the old man barked out a laugh. "Let me just say, that if I get the slightest opportunity, I'm going to peel the flesh off both of you and suck on it like candy."

James reached for another item on the desk, his hand hovering.

"Okay, all right," the old man said. "No reason to get testy."

James sat back. "I want information. Not scraps. Not one question, I want all the information, and I want it now," James said.

"And if I refuse?" the old man said.

"Then we go back and likely die and you spend eternity wondering what getting out of here might have been like."

"My kind holds information dearly. We have already agreed that you will show me the basement. What do you have that I would want beyond that?"

"We have yet to agree on exactly when," James said.

"When then?" the old man asked.

"Within the hour," James replied.

The old man's tongue flickered out. The crow spread its wings lazily.

"Don't ever play poker," James said. "By the way, that's an hour there, not here." he concluded.

The old man turned to Ellen. "And you. Will you be the one to do it?"

Ellen shifted in her seat. "Sure, why not?"

"With your guts spilling onto the dirt floor and your lungs full of bloody fish bones, you'll still do it?"

Ellen shifted again. "You'll come when I call you," she said.

"Will I?" it smiled. "Across the ache of time and the surging tides of meat, a journey I cannot make alone, in all my knowledge and power?"

Ellen set her jaw. "You'll come," she said. "If I called that one, I can call you."

"I told you, you didn't call it," the old man said, smiling, the grey flesh on its face cracking again. "It noticed you. Like an insect is ever noticed."

"Well then notice me when I call you," Ellen finished.

The old man turned back to James; its hands open. "How can I help?" it said.

"Who are they? Why are they still on that ship?" James said.

A great leather-bound book was on the desk. *Had it been there moments before?* The old man opened the book and turned it around to face them. His finger descended to point to a drawing on the stained yellow page. It was a ship's outline, seen from above.

Inside the outline of the ship, hundreds of bodies were drawn packed in orderly rows, cargo, side by side. The old man's eyes glittered with malice.

Ellen let out a soft moan, her fingertips at her lips. James visibly sank back.

"The slavers filled the sea with the bodies of their cargo, the dead and the dying. They threw thousands overboard for hundreds of years. Their captives died in so many different ways, chained below decks in the dark for weeks. Smallpox, diphtheria, dehydration, starvation, beatings, despair."

"The girl," James said.

"They won't leave her," the old man said. "And the one like me, down there? It won't let her go."

Ellen was gathering herself. Finally, she spoke.

"Children. Over and over, they keep asking someone to help them," She sighed. A hint of fear rose, far off. Like a distant church bell. Anywhere else, the idea of going back down into the basement would induce panic, but here, in this place, the idea was able to take hold for her. She visualized the small hand in hers, so fierce. The ship rolling slowly on the waves of the vast ocean. The sounds of so many others, a chorus of chains rattling.

"We can't leave her, Jimmy."

"Hm," he said. He glanced across at her, deep sadness in his eyes. *For this thing, I am deeply sorry.* He looked back at the old man. "Why do they leave her alone, but want me dead?" James asked.

"So many secrets. You want to tell him or should I?" the old man said.

James looked to Ellen. She returned his gaze. "Oh," James said. He dropped his head for a moment. "That's how you got so good at hiding what you are," James said.

Ellen shrugged. "I was born with this skin. I can pass as white. When my mother was murdered and I came to my father's house, I just stepped into his world. The price of course is now I belong nowhere," she said.

"Deceiver," the old man said.

"Ah, yes. Deceiver. Your favorite word," James said to the old man. "What lies do you tell yourself, you sack of other people's suffering? Shut the fuck up."

"Can we trust it?" Ellen asked James.

"I'm sitting right here," the old man said. "Why not ask me?"

Ellen turned to face it. "Can we trust you to help us when we call you?"

"You can trust me to help myself," the old man replied.

"And what will that look like?" Ellen asked.

The old man stroked his red and bloody chin. "I can't say as I remember."

"Remember what?"

"What I was before all of these," the old man said waving his hand toward the endless shelves of books around him.

"Hm," James said.

Ellen looked towards him.

"They're not books," James said.

She looked back toward the old man. "What are they?"

"I think you know," the old man smiled.

Ellen looked at the book open before them. The bodies diagrammed neatly inside the boat's hull, drawn with efficient clarity, an instruction manual, or perhaps for ease of accounting. She put her hand forward.

"You don't want that thread," the old man said, his voice

strangely soft. "It is a level of sin that… is difficult to get free of."

James barked out a short laugh. "That one, in the basement, is angry. But you, you eat sin."

"A completely different kind of trap devouring sin," the old man replied. "One starts off feeling justified. But that's not how any of it ends up. That one in the basement? It stays because it is full of rage. I stay because they have bound me." It waved his hand to the books. "If you call me out of here, I will be free of them. I may even become what I was. That thing which I cannot remember. But can you call me away from all of these, insect?" it said to Ellen. "We shall see, I suppose." It turned to James. "In an hour you say?"

"Yes, but one more set of questions," James replied.

The old man sucked on its teeth. "In for a penny," it said.

"The other one. Can you beat him?"

The old man let out a dry laugh. "Of course not. That one is an ancient, a leviathan from the lowest places of the sea. It was made before time for the dreaming of the world. Never meant to be woken. But men woke the tiniest part of it with their incalculable cruelty and as I am diminished, so that tiniest fraction of the leviathan is diminished, held by its dark appetites. You cannot imagine how small a part of it is actually awake, but enough to crush what I am in a heartbeat," the old man said gleefully.

"Then what difference will it make calling for you?" Ellen asked.

"There is a small chance," the old man said.

"Of what?" James replied.

"That what I once was is something greater than what you see now," the old man said sheepishly. "Then maybe I can buy you a minute of time. Or I may tear you both to pieces. Who can say?"

178

James turned. "We have to go back and finish it," he said.

"All right. Just a few minutes longer," she replied.

"Look for me to return," James said to the old man. "Possibly a hundred times as the next hour plays out. However long I'm here, stay out of my way. You don't want me dead before we call for you."

The old man smiled, or perhaps grimaced, as thin rivulets of blood ran shining down its face.

Ellen picked herself up off the porch. James was there next to her. All the fear in her body patiently waiting for her return was hammering away at her. Her mind slightly detached, struggled to firewall off her body's drowning terror. "God damn it," she said.

"Don't I know it," James said. He went back to the rail and vomited again. He looked up, long rivulets dripping from his mouth. The family from before was passing the other way.

"Don't look," the father said, hurrying his children along.

James turned, sitting back down next to Ellen.

"Are we really bringing the crow here?" she asked.

"I hope not," James said. "If we can just release the girl, that will untangle it all."

"Right," Ellen said looking away.

"I'll be with you," James said.

She was silent. "I know, it's just …" her voice trailed off. I don't know if I'm enough. If I can last … um, hold on." Ellen shifted uncomfortably. She ran her hands up and down her upper arms, seeking to comfort herself. Jimmy waited, watching her.

"The last time," she said. "I touched her, her pain came into me. I fell apart instantly. I couldn't hold space for her for half a second. All my training was useless. I didn't last for an instant. Not for a moment. I fought like an animal to get away from her. That's what I did. I just fought to get away from her. She knew. To my everlasting shame, I saw it on her face."

Ellen looked up at Jimmy, tears falling freely. "She looked so … puzzled. Just supremely confused by me. Why did I come to her only to leave her there? She's blind, I think. Just … reaching out and I fought to get away. That's what I did."

James sat with her in the silence that followed.

Ellen shook her head. "I don't want that pain. I don't do well with pain that hurts like that, you know?"

And she looked up. James was watching her, his eyes aglow, shocking blue.

"Like what?" he asked.

"Like children hurt," she said.

"Me neither," he said. And tears welled up in his eyes. She watched them spill freely down his face, momentarily surprised and then curious why such a thing should surprise her. She put her hand on his arm.

"Yeah, me neither," she echoed him.

They sat together for the next few hours. Their backs to the wall beneath the windows. Their forearms laying side by side, their fingers gently interlaced. They watched the changing of the light.

The sun was setting when they finally rose to stand side by side before the door of the great house, still holding hands. For those with eyes to see, a third figure was there as well, standing stiff and cold a few feet apart. A woman dressed in her white burial dress, her expression dead and emotionless, gazing at them with sightless, blank eyes. One hand clasping and unclasping.

Ellen pushed open the door to the house and she and James

stepped into the entry hall. The low-angled sun cast patches of gold across the rooms around them.

James glanced toward the front room, feeling an unexpected twinge of nostalgia. The two couches were there, pushed to opposite ends of the room. Ellen's laptop was where she had left it. He took in the entry hall, glancing up the stairs to the floor above. For a fleeting moment, it conjured for him the sense of what having a home might feel like.

He shook off the feeling and looked at Ellen. She nodded yes. They took a firmer grip on each other's hands and began walking down the long hallway. The floor creaked as they advanced, moving past the dining room. The patterns of light on the walls formed the briefest distraction. And then they passed through the doorway and into the kitchen. He recalled the last time he had passed through that doorway, roughly propelled, surrounded by the violent men. Again, a twinge of nostalgia, an old story from long ago. They walked toward the couch in the breakfast nook and Ellen turned toward him. There was fear, but also something else, difficult to name, that made them communicate by looks alone.

Ellen drew the tiniest intake of sharp breath. James looked over his shoulder. There at the basement doorway stood the girl, shadows roiling about her.

There was the sound of wood splitting and squealing. The floor broke open and Ellen fell through into the basement, her hand ripped from James' in an instant. The last thing he saw was her eyes wide with surprise. He rushed toward the basement door and the flies descended on him, so vast a number that all light and vision was instantly blotted out.

Ellen hit the basement floor, turning her ankle. The pain was instant and sharp. The room was utterly dark but for the light filtering down from the kitchen above.

"Jimmy!" she yelled. Then she heard it from above, the drone of flies, so many of them. "Oh, my god," she said under her breath. "Jimmy! I'm coming!" She stumbled forward out of the pool of light into the deep darkness, heading for where she knew the stairs to be. She found the wall, feeling for the light switch at the bottom of the stairs. She flipped it on and there stood the ranks of the dead all about her. And something else toward the back of the basement. Something vast, radiating long tendrils of bleak luminescence; cold pale malice. Something that was reaching for her again; a trembling shock of recognition lashed through her, the damage engulfing her. In a panic, she pictured the crow and said, "Come."

And it did not come. "Come," she cried again, terror threading though her voice now. The thing was closer. Not so much physically but in the way a bad dream is suddenly deeply intimate when it takes a turn for the worse. A great invisible hand descended on her. In an utterly alien languid motion, she found herself pressed down to the basement floor, held there. She glanced about her.

"I'm sorry ... " she cried out, the air sliding away, rasping. Was she speaking to James or to the girl? Perhaps both.

The thing moved closer; the bodies of the dead brushed aside; blades of grass as a storm moves. It was there, a moment more away, rising above her.

Then James began to descend the stairs. She turned her head, his footfalls coming slowly, falling strange and robotic on the wooden treads. First, she saw only his feet, the harsh lightbulb at the bottom of the stairs blinding her to detail, but his feet looked too big, too blocky. He descended further and his knees, waist,

182

chest were revealed. All strangely blocky, too big.

He's covered in flies. She struggled fiercely to rise. "Aaaaahhhhhh!" she screamed pushing up to her knees. "Stop!" she screamed. "Stop hurting him!" Jimmy reached the base of the stairs. He turned; his head now fully illuminated by the light. His face was hidden in a thick layer of swarming, biting flies, many inches deep, moving and boiling about, each insect in a frenzy to reach flesh, to take blood.

Ellen could not stay upright. She collapsed back to the floor, struggling to rise all over again. She watched in horror as James walked slowly, mechanically toward her. *Is he even alive?* she thought. "Jimmy!" she screamed, fighting to rise again.

He walked past her and stopped. The leviathan rose above him now, the angry droning of the flies quieting a bit. There was a stuttering in the room, as if light, sound, air, walls, time, and meaning all flashed impermanent, flickering. Ellen heard or felt something seismic happen not only to the earth beneath her, but also to the stars above, flung outside across the night sky. And then, just as suddenly as it had come, the force holding her down was gone. She rose and took a step toward Jimmy. He held out his hand toward her palm out, flies roiling across the obscured flesh. A clear signal. *Stop.* Then she became aware of something behind her. She started to turn and look when she heard his voice, calm and clear above the drone of the flies. "Ellen, you need to get out of the way."

She moved quickly to the wall beneath the stairs. It was then she saw the bear. So much greater than the simple confines of the basement. Crouched, its mountainous shoulders towering above the first floor of the house itself, a thing of hot blood, some small part of it in this world but most well beyond it. Its eyes glowed with red fire. Stars rained down off its fur, bouncing lightly onto the basement floor. Its breath rolled like a drum, an unending earthy rumble that fed an energy of precise and focused power into the room.

"Help the girl," James said turning slowly back to face the leviathan and the bear roared. It was a terrible sound. Ellen found she had pressed her hands to her ears. There was a moment of stillness. Then James whispered a word she could not hear. With that, the great beast charged past Ellen and slammed into the leviathan, raining stars as it went.

And the girl was there. Ellen saw her just a few steps away, arms reaching out, fully visible. All around the girl, some half hidden in the walls, figures stood slightly apart from the child, creating a half circle about her.

James was making a heart-rending sound. He stood strangely still to her right, flies boiling over him. A scream would start to rise from him and then stop, like an audio tape paused. Then it would start again and stop. Then it would start again, and stop instantly, looping like some truncated torture, repeating over and over.

It was then that Ellen realized. *He's going back and forth to the Crow's library. Using it to recover. No time passes here but there....* Beyond James, the great bear was being torn apart, stars raining down as it was dismembered by the leviathan.

Ellen made her way across to the girl, stars spilling across the floor around her feet. "I'm sorry," she whispered. "I'm sorry I left you alone, but I'm here now." She was reaching out for the girl when the stars stopped falling. The bear was finished, savagely torn to pieces, shimmering on the floor of the basement. It struggled to look back towards James who still stood stock still, and its eyes went dark. The leviathan came forward and enveloped James entirely. But as it did so, James turned, patches of his bloodied skin visible, his face supremely calm, his eyes glowing like stars. In the last possible moment, he flung out his hand, and across the space between them the scarab flew end over end.

For this thing, I am deeply sorry.

Ellen caught the scarab. There was a detonation inside of her, some million things died, some million things were born. She saw James collapse into the void that was the leviathan and her anger at every cruelty ever inflicted sang in her, a single bright chord. She pictured the crow, held it fast in her anger and grief, turned it over in her loss and despair, gave it solidity and purpose in her rage. Raising her hand above her, she looked down at the child standing naked before her, tortured in white hot agonies, her child's neck swollen shut, her eyes blinded, her arms out, hungry, her hope for help transcendent, and Ellen called out.

"Come!"

And something came.

It came from behind her. Traveling, lightning to the rain-soaked earth, moving with such speed that she saw only the end of its passing. It was a thing of pure light, scattering darkness as if darkness had never existed. It rattled the cage of reality and broke it cleanly, taking the leviathan with it down the long corridor of time, opening up worlds beyond worlds. Ellen saw what James had seen, the entire length of the ship and an eternity of some distant realm beyond it. There was the sound of successive detonations, increasingly distant as the leviathan and what had been the crow transited away across time, the universe, everything that is.

Ellen turned back to the girl, dropped to one knee, embraced her, and the basement was gone.

There was a smell. Things rotting. Absolute darkness. She looked around herself, unable to pierce her blindness. Locked down again, at her wrists and legs. A small hand in hers, fiercely holding on. A slow shifting beneath her. She drifted in a sea of white-hot pain. So much darkness, never any light.

"I'm here," James said from somewhere in that darkness.

The mass of flies that covered James had become tinted red. As they boiled over his body, fighting to burrow down to his flesh, they had angrily stirred his blood throughout the mass of them. They were reluctantly dissipating, as if finally tasting him, they were unwilling to give up their feast. But James was carrying Ellen up and out of the basement. One slow step at a time he went, still robotic, transiting back and forth, over and over, between the terror and panic of the present and the calm silent library of the Crow. Every step he took, prepared for in the now abandoned library, perhaps for a minute, an hour, or a day; who could say? One slow step at a time, he carried Ellen up the groaning stairs. Step by step, they emerged into the blinding, sunlit brightness of the kitchen.

Wasn't.

The.

Sun.

Setting?

The flies gone, his face and forearms bloody red, James turned robotically toward the side door that led outside. He drew the door open and went out, holding her. Along the side of the house, he walked with her, his steps finally falling into a normal cadence. He carried her to a patch of grass in the overgrown back yard, nearby roses planted by a dead woman moving in the morning breeze.

James laid Ellen gently on the grass and took her hand. "I'm here," he said to her, and she opened her eyes.

She looked up into a mass of sunlit leaves moving gently above her. James was lit in morning light, red and bloody, his eyes glowing blue like twin stars. He gestured to her side. Curled up in the crook of her arm was the girl. Sores everywhere across the child's body, her neck swollen like a bull's and rash red. The same terrible sores were appearing on Ellen's skin, swarming in waves, marching in ranks across her body. Ellen made a small sound. The sound of surprise when pain is revealed to be so immense.

She drew the child closer. The pain increased. Something was expanding in her throat, shutting off the cool morning air, hot and painful. The sound of Ellen's breathing became a struggle, with something new underneath. Liquid in her lungs, a gurgling sound as she fought to draw air. The leaves above her moved gently.

The child next to her made the smallest of sounds, surprise also. Now half blind, Ellen turned slowly to look. The child's skin was unblemished, her neck small and elegant. She was looking at Ellen, her eyes reflecting deep sympathy, *an apology?*

"No, no, baby," Ellen whispered, her voice a rasping gurgle, the sores swarming across her face. Then the child began to shimmer. A soft light and she was gone. Ellen felt the pain go with her, instantly just a memory. She stared up into the green leaves above her, moving in the gentle breezes. James continued to hold her hand.

"They're gone," he said from somewhere far away.

Epilogue

Ellen and James sat side by side on the porch step. Morning commuters moved by on the sidewalk. Weeks had passed. James' skin was well on its way to healing. The scarring would remain. Ellen wore her professional attire. An afternoon worth of clients awaited her, her colleagues glad that the predictable cadence of their lives again included her, even if she seemed a bit ... different.

She stood and took in the day as it spread itself out before her, her leather bag strapped neatly across her shoulder. She took a few steps down the stairs and looked back up at Jimmy.

"You got anything going today?" she said, smiling.

James held a coffee cup in his hands. "Guy in Oakland. Says there's something weird in the back seat of his car," he said with a shrug.

"Okay, well, have fun," she said. She walked out the gate. Her hand made a little flourish above her head. "Don't bring any unwanted guests home," she said, laughing as she disappeared into the throng of morning commuters. Jimmy sat and watched her go. He noted the lightness in her step as she went. Then he set his cup on the porch, rose, descended the steps and walked out the gate.

There was an aquarium on one side of the waiting room. Rainbow-colored fish moved in slow circles as the water gently circulated. Women of all ages came and went around Ellen.

A woman at the front desk received them as they entered, inviting them to sit, to relax for a moment before their appointments.

A woman in her seventies came toward Ellen down the long hallway. Her hair was white as snow. She wore a colorful dress cut simply. Glasses hung from a chain at her neck. Ellen watched her approaching, a smile slowly spreading across each of their faces. Ellen stood to greet her.

"Ellen," the woman said, her voice warm and clear.

Ellen stepped forward and they embraced.

"Thank you for agreeing to see me," Ellen said.

"One of my most promising interns? How could I resist? Just to find out what you're up to," she laughed. "Come this way."

Ellen followed the woman down the hall, the woman's shoulders upright and resolute as she walked. She gestured for Ellen to enter her office, a picture of wildflowers half visible on the wall inside. She followed Ellen in and gently closed the door.

James entered a garage attached to a big house in the Oakland hills. A trim well-dressed middle-aged man walked behind him, hesitant. There were half a dozen cars side by side down the length of the long well-lit space, not a single drop of oil anywhere on the pristine cement floor.

James walked past a Ferrari, a Bentley, and a 1930s Packard Sedan. He stopped in front of a 1939 Volkswagen Beetle. The man with him had dropped back several yards. James opened the passenger side door and sat down in the seat. He left the door hanging wide open. He fiddled with the knobs on the dash for a moment, smiling, took out a cigarette and lit it. He exhaled long plumes of tobacco smoke, his expression that of a man casually waiting for bus or a train.

He cocked his head sideways. He dropped the cigarette outside the car and ground it out with his foot. Then he slowly turned to look over his shoulder at the back seat, his eyes glowing shocking blue.

"Well look at you," he said.

About the Author

Mark Greene was born and raised in Texas. He lives in New York City with his wife and son. *Voices in the Ghost Light* is the second novel in his James Hatch series. *Dance of the Hanged Man* is the first.

www.ingramcontent.com/pod-product-compliance
Lightning Source LLC
Chambersburg PA
CBHW071204260626
47162CB00003B/1165